Double
Dutch

A Salt Mine Novel

Joseph Browning   Suzi Yee

Text Copyright © 2021 by Joseph Browning and Suzi Yee

Published by Expeditious Retreat Press
Cover by J Caleb Design
Edited by Elizabeth VanZwoll

For information regarding Joseph Browning and Suzi Yee:

Subscribe to their mailing list at their website: https://www.joseph-browning.com

To follow them on Twitter: https://twitter.com/Joseph_Browning

To follow Joseph on Facebook: https://www.facebook.com/joseph.browning.52

To follow Suzi on Facebook: https://www.facebook.com/SuziYeeAuthor/

To follow them on MeWe: https://mewe.com/i/josephbrowning

By Joseph Browning and Suzi Yee

THE SALT MINE NOVELS

Money Hungry	Hen Pecked	Dark Matter
Feeding Frenzy	Brain Drain	Silent Night
Ground Rules	Bone Dry	Deep Sleep
Mirror Mirror	Vicious Circle	Home Grown
Bottom Line	High Horse	Better Half
Whip Smart	Fair Game	Mortal Coil
Rest Assured	Double Dutch	

Chapter One

Heiderscheidergrund, Luxembourg
2nd of September, 1:41 a.m. (GMT+2)

The Sûre River coiled like a snake among the forested hills of the Ardennes, sinuously sliding from cut bank to point bar as it whittled away at the bedrock. A black inflatable boat glided in the languid current, steered by two men with paddles in hand. At the vessel's front and center was a third man scanning the area with night vision binoculars.

All three were dressed in clothes as dark as the boat. From a distance, they formed a mass that was indistinguishable from a large log floating downstream in the middle of a dim and drizzly night. That was their directive: keep a low profile. No one was supposed to know where they had been or notice that anything was missing after they had come and gone. Their cover was three Russians vacationing in scenic Luxembourg, a country littered with fortifications dating back to the Middle Ages.

When Ivory Tower triad leader Lieutenant Konan Lokhov spotted the towers of their destination in his binoculars, he held up a gloved hand and signaled a direction. His juniors slowly dipped their oars into the smooth water, setting a course for the verdant green beneath.

The silhouette of the castle stood tall on the forested slope of a strategic piece of ground. *Schlass Wollef* lorded over one of the large meanders of the Sûre, cutting off the neck of the peninsula with a massive stone wall linked by a rampart to the main body of the castle. Bearing resemblance to a stone wolf in sphinxlike repose, its upright ear-like towers were perpetually on alert.

Built in 1189 by the French—then christened Château du Loup—it was little more than a rough and brutal structure spartanly filled with crude necessities used to extract tolls from the river traffic under threat of violence. As the coffers of greater Europe swelled with all the goods that swords, guns, and cannons could procure, Schlass Wollef too grew in refinement but its brutality never diminished, even in all its finery.

As they made land, the PVC bottom scraped against the pebbles of the shoreline. Lokhov let the binoculars drape around his neck as he exited and pulled the boat a little further inland to make the way easier for the others. His flat, angular face was unchanged despite the exertions, and the two younger men stowed their paddles and dragged the boat completely out of the water.

Anatoly Kirpichenko was the youngest of the triad and given the lowly task of securing the raft. He made no complaint of the grunt work. At the tender age of seventeen, he was simply glad to be out of the classroom and into the field. He was recruited by the Ivory Tower four years ago when scouting agents passed through the schools of Igrim. When they recognized his unusual talents, a deal was struck. For the price of 30,000 rubles a month for five years, his parents agreed to give wardship of him to the state; such opportunities rarely reached east of the Urals.

He was trained in tradecraft and hand-to-hand combat as well as weaponry, and it had taken years to erase his rural accent and teach him English, Spanish, and Latin, which he needed in his magical studies. Part of his education was instilling a sense of pride and superiority. He was the elite of Russia, destined for great things provided he was loyal to his superiors and followed their orders. It hadn't been easy, but Kirpichenko emerged as hard as the rocks he used to weigh down the boat.

Lokhov took point as they ascended, ever aware of the position of his subordinates. In addition to his mission objective, Lokhov was also tasked with the field training of the other two members of the triad. Like himself, Junior Lieutenant Petr Stashkysnky was former SVR, but he was relatively new to the Ivory Tower. Lokhov didn't have to worry about his spycraft, but Stashkysnky's arcane ability was a different matter.

Kirpichenko was completely green, the first generation of the Ivory Tower's new recruiting process. Instead of looking for soldiers and spies that could be trained to use magic, they sought pubescent magicians and trained them for service. It was a move toward custom-tailored operatives with no previous institutional loyalties, which sounded great on paper but in the field meant that training became an even steeper learning curve. This was only Kirpichenko's third mission and Lokhov kept a close watch on the rookie's every move.

They wended up the steep incline in single file using the trees for cover. The drizzle hadn't penetrated the canopy and the dry exposed roots made adequate handholds as they crossed the uneven ground. Buried under the lush greenery were all the divots and shell holes from the bloody and relentless battles between the Allies and the Axis along the river decades ago. The foliage softened the scars, but they were still visible to the observant, like the keen eyes of a doctor sussing out where a bone once broken had healed.

As they cleared the tree line, the stone wall towered forty feet above them—a weathered stoic face pockmarked with 800 years of attack from nature and man. The last ten feet to the wall was extremely rocky, a holdover from the castle's original defense. Even after hundreds of years of exposure, the ring of sharp and jagged rubble was still difficult to cross without twisting or cutting an ankle.

When they made it to the base of the wall, Stashkysnky unfolded a small grappling hook and lobbed it over the side. His eye followed its trajectory as it sailed over and onto the other side of the steel safety railing—a modern precaution installed on the interior of the wall-walk to prevent the vapid flock of tourists from falling into the courtyard. The sound of the grapple hitting metal rang out in the night despite its thin noise-reducing rubber coating. With a practiced touch, Stashkysnky carefully pulled on the knotted rope until he felt the hook catch and hold, and the three shadows made their way up the wall.

They gained the wall-walk with ease and crouched low as Stashkysnky retrieved the grappling hook and Lokhov secured his dangling binoculars in his backpack. As Stashkysnky folded it flat and hurriedly coiled the rope, Kirpichenko stole a peek from the top. "It's not the fall that kills you. It's the landing," Lokhov said deadpan in Russian, slowly zipping up his backpack. Stashkysnky smirked as he returned the hook and rope to his pack.

When they reached the end of the public wall-walk they encountered a small metal barrier, the only indication they had reached the private section of the castle that was off limits to the daily public tours. The men easy circumvented the perfunctory barrier as it was little more than a "Do Not Enter" sign—a polite warning that wasn't engineered to keep anyone determined out.

They followed the wall to a thick wooden door. From previous days of reconnoitering, they knew there were no on-site guards and all the security cameras were pointed at locations where money exchanged hands and the designated public entrances. The only thing they had to worry about was magical protection.

Lokhov gathered his will and smeared it across the door and threshold like spackle on a wall. There were a few wards against fae and fiends, but they had faded with the death of their caretaker, the recently departed Graaf Hendrik van der Meer. Picking the old-fashioned lock posed absolutely no challenge and the trio waited patiently on the other side until Lokhov closed the well-oiled door behind them before turning on their flashlights.

Their three beams revealed a long hall decorated with several suits of armor, including a set of full barding for a horse. Opposite the armor were medieval weapons separated by type and hung upon the wall in starburst formations with narrow tapestries in between. Lokhov lead the way down the corridor to the next, which was bedecked with paintings of considerable age and skill. Generations of van de Meers haughtily stared down their sharp noses at the three as they passed. The wealth on display was impressive, but that wasn't their objective. What they needed was in the library.

Unfortunately, they weren't exactly sure how to get there. While much of the lower levels of the castle were part of the tour, whole sections of the lower levels and all of the upper levels were the private residence of the great family that had built Schlass Wollef—a convoluted lineage that could trace back to the Holy Roman Empress Cunigunde of Luxembourg. There were no public building schematics of the entire castle to tell them how to get from here to there, and the directions extracted through interrogation lacked GPS precision.

After two wrong turns, they finally arrived at the large three-storied rectangular hall filled with row upon row of books. The central atrium stretched from the reading tables on the ground floor to the rib-vaulted, glass-paned ceiling. After orienting themselves, the Russians circled the third floor in search of a Carlton House desk. They moved quietly on the thick carpet. Even though Kirpichenko was taking the same path as the others, he seemed to find every loose floorboard. When Stashkysnky joked they should call him "squeaky," Lokhov motioned for operational silence but laughed to himself.

They paused when Lokhov directed his beam to the pale creamy ash desk with cherry and ebony inlay. He scanned it with his will and frowned. It wasn't supposed to be magically trapped or locked, yet here it was. "When a magician is involved, always scan it," he whispered, turning this unexpected development into a teaching moment. "Tell me, what do you see?"

Stashkysnky threw his will together. "It's magically locked," he answered.

Kirpichenko, who was more in tune with practicing the arts, had a more discerning eye. "And trapped," he added.

Not to be outdone by the whelp, Stashkysnky concentrated harder. "With a fear ward on the drawers."

"Quite effective, given how close the edge is," Lokhov pointed to the railings and the two-story drop. "But you both missed the subtle apathy ward on the desk in general. Anyone touching it will immediately lose interest in it, and only the more determined are subjected to the fear." He gave them a second to appreciate the craftsmanship before proceeding.

"I'm going to disarm it, but it is complex. Prepare yourself in case I fail," Lokhov warned them. Only he would be subject to the apathy ward, but the fear could radiate. If the ward hit them hard enough, fear could drive them over the railing with disastrous consequences.

The triad leader gathered his will and twisted it through the ward. He needed to reach the center knot and connect to the interior binding without touching any other part, not unlike the children's game *Operation*.

He made it halfway through when he clipped a corner and triggered the ward. All three felt a wave of fear wash over them, but Lokhov bore the brunt of it. He grunted like he'd taken a punch to the gut, but he held his ground. Behind him, he heard Stashkysnky whimper and Kirpichenko yelp. When he looked over his shoulder, the junior lieutenant was still in position but the rookie had taken a few steps back.

"Brace yourself, I'm going in for another pass," Lokhov murmured. On his second attempt, he got three-fourths of the way through before triggering the ward. This time the triad stood strong against the magic. Now that they knew what they were up against, there were no balled fists or shaky legs. Instead of reflexively recoiling in fear, Lokhov kept steady hold of his will. Rather than have to start over from the beginning, he advanced his will the rest of the way.

When he finally hit the sweet spot, the esoteric bands around the desk suddenly dropped. He missed the tactile sense of release that came from picking physical locks but grinned at his success nonetheless. He gave a thumbs-up to his men to let them know they were back on track.

With the magical lock disarmed, all that was left was the mechanical one cleverly built into the desk. If the interrogation intel was correct, the eight drawers functioned as pins of a lock to a panel disguised as a section of inlay, and their mission objective lay within the hidden compartment behind it.

One by one, the triad leader opened the drawers in the proper sequence. When the last was partially opened, there was not just one audible click, but two. Both were overshadowed by a small flat package falling from the underside of the desk and belly flopping on the floor.

The younger men directed their beams at the fallen package, but Lokhov kept his focus on the mission. With his gloved hand, he pushed the panel aside and extracted a velvet bag. He loosened its strings and examined the large silver signet ring that fell into his hand: the lion of Luxembourg was etched into the carnelian set in its bezel. He placed it back into its plush sachet and secured that in the waterproof pouch that hung around his neck.

Only then did he turn his attention to the plastic bag on the floor. He brought it to the desk for inspection. The bag was modern but its contents were older. Wrapped in conservator cloth was a small booklet containing sixteen pages. It was rectangular—larger than a postcard but smaller than a sheet of printer paper. Colorful illustrations dotted the carefully inked letters written on the vellum. Lokhov was no expert, but it looked medieval to him. He tried to read it but he didn't recognize any words, even though it looked like Latin.

"What do we do with that?" Stashkysnky asked from behind.

The directive had been clear: take nothing except the ring. No one was to suspect anything had been removed, and anyone that might have noticed the ring was missing was already dead. The SVR had seen to that. But the triad leader figured this manuscript had to be important if it was kept under the same protections as the ring. It was worthy of inquiry.

"We ask and if we get no answer, we follow the brief," Lokhov answered as he pulled out his phone. It was the kind of lesson that wasn't in the books or taught in classes: show initiative but cover your ass. He took a few pictures to include with his message to his commander: *primary objective obtained. Potential second objective found during recovery. Please advise.*

He noted the time and decided to give it five minutes. While he waited, he carefully enclosed the pages in the silk cloth and placed it back in its bag. Then, he crawled under the desk to take a closer look at where the pages had been kept in case there was something else stashed inside that hadn't succumbed to gravity.

On his back with flashlight in hand, Lokhov patted down the compartment. After he found it empty, he started fiddling with the moving parts; regardless of the booklet's fate, it would have to be sealed before they left. He'd just about figured it out when his phone vibrated in his pocket: *Bring it in.*

He sent back a single word—*Understood*—before resetting the secret compartments and securing the package in his backpack. "We're done here. Stashkysnky, close it up."

The junior lieutenant shut the drawers in reverse sequence. As the final drawer closed, the magic of the wards returned and his respect for Lokhov rose as he caught a hint of the apathy the triad leader had shrugged off earlier. Satisfied, the Russians doubled back in silence, unaware of the fourth shadow they had acquired.

Chapter Two

Aaron Haddock—codename Stigma—took cover when he heard someone else enter the library's upper story. He wasn't expecting company and stayed hidden as he counted three figures pass by. In the lead was a thick man of average height followed by a short slim man and a tall lithe one, all dressed in black like himself. When he heard them speak Russian, he suspected the Ivory Tower, who favored sending triads.

Haddock's assignment was simple: recover the magical books from the library after the demise of Graaf Hendrik van der Meer. The van der Meer's were the last branch that could inherit the ancestral property of the van Verdun family, a linage that was once broad and long. Unfortunately, the current graaf died without issue. The Salt Mine had sent in Haddock to collect the enchanted writings—if there were any—before everything became property of the state, where they could fall into the wrong hands or endanger unwitting people.

From the shadows, he watched the triad move and quickly surmised that they weren't here to browse as they made a beeline for the magical desk on the northeast side of the atrium. He'd already made note of it and taken pictures for Chloe and Dot. It was too large to take with him, but if the twins thought it was something worth the effort, it could be bought at auction or liberated at a later time. Of course, he'd checked the drawers after bypassing the magical wards, but they were empty of anything interesting.

He placed the three men in pecking order after watching their interactions. He wryly smiled when the leader fumbled his disarm attempt. When the thick-necked Russian tripped the desk's ward, Haddock silently angled for a better vantage point in the panic. None of them seemed aware of his presence yet and he readied his will in case that changed and to ward against another potential failure on their part. He gave the Russian even odds of failing again and this time he suspected he'd be close enough to be affected by the desk's projections.

The triad held themselves together better the second time, and the fear rolled over Haddock like water off a duck's back. When the triad leader finally disarmed the desk, He noted the odd order in which he opened the drawers. *What do they know that I don't*, he wondered to himself. He quickly crafted a visual mnemonic to remember the sequence.

He saw a plastic-wrapped package fall from the desk's underside, but that wasn't the first thing the triad leader grabbed. He could see the cloth bag the Russian had pulled out from behind the secret panel but not its contents. He kept it close, like a poker player holding his cards to his chest. Whatever it was, it was back in its sachet and in the leader's neck pouch before Haddock could ease the hag stone from his pocket to see if it was magical.

He cursed his missed opportunity but didn't make the same mistake twice. He held the smooth stone to his eye and looked through the naturally bored hole as they unwrapped the slim package that had fallen out of the desk. Even in the dark, the color seemed to drain from the world and gravitate toward the object on the desk. It was definitely enchanted and, in an instant, he decided there was no way he could let the Ivory Tower have it although it wasn't really in his operation's parameters. The fact that they knew about it, where it was located in the castle, how to open up the trick desk, *and* that they'd sent a full triad to pick it up tipped the scales of his judgement. Whatever it was, they valued it so he wanted to take it away.

He put the hag stone away and ran through his options. If it were mano a mano, he wouldn't hesitate to attack, but he was outnumbered three to one. Even with the element of surprise and his superior practice of magic—with few exceptions, Ivory Tower agents weren't known for their magical prowess—the odds of him taking all three out in a direct assault were slim. Which meant he had to be dastardly about it.

While the Russians were taking pictures and resetting the secret compartments, Haddock mentally did a quick inventory.

The special equipment given him by Harold Weber, the Mine's resident quartermaster, was directed toward the mission: a hag stone, a vape pen saltcaster, and a book safe esoterically refitted by the German himself. Weber had added shelves, making the hollowed-out space a miniature bookshelf that could carry up to fifty books, including magical ones, within the false covers. It was ideal for a retrieval mission but hardly helpful in combat.

Fortunately, Haddock always kept additional gear on him, magically tattooed on his skin—basic survival tools as well as an assortment of weapons inked on just in case. There was a sharp hunting knife along each calf, a loaded pistol on one forearm and a pair of crossed Louisville Sluggers on the other.

Optics demanded discretion, so whatever move he made, it needed to be outside. Dead bodies and blood in the library would attract attention, and he didn't want anyone to know he was inside Schlass Wollef after-hours. He stuck to the walls and crept around corners as he followed the triad's flashlights in the otherwise dark castle. When they exited onto the upper bailey, he gave them a little time to move on before cracking the door on its blessedly well-maintained hinges.

The Russians were nowhere in sight, but he heard them. The triad leader gave Stashkysnky, who Haddock now knew to be the short slim one, an order to secure the grappling hook and take point. He took cover behind the metal barrier and poked just enough of his head out to get a visual: Stashkysnky circled the metal end of the grappling hook around the safety railing before throwing the rope down the outer castle wall. Haddock smiled at his good fortune. The gold standard in state-sanctioned murder was making it look natural, and there wasn't anything more natural than gravity.

Haddock gathered his will and waited for his moment. Stashkysnky tugged on the line to make sure it was secure before sliding through the crenellations and over the edge. Once his head dipped below the wall, Haddock brought his will upon the nylon rope, cleanly slicing through it. Stashkysnky screamed but his shriek abruptly ended with a sickening thump as he landed on the rocky rubble below.

Haddock squeezed through the gap to the other side of the metal barrier as Stashkysnky's two comrades stretched themselves over the thick battlements to see what had happened.

"Petr!" the triad leader whisper-shouted but there was no answer.

"He's not moving," the other one said in a panic.

Haddock closed the distance and lifted the lithe one's legs up and pushed out. Unprepared for the shift in weight, Kirpichenko lost his balance and bellowed loudly once he realized he was falling. His black silhouette smashed next to Stashkysnky's, their arms almost around each other.

Lokhov's training took over and instead of looking down, he looked behind him and caught a shadow out of the corner of his eye. Despite his ungainly position halfway over the battlement, he kicked and made contact.

Haddock grunted as he took a hit to the chest. With the element of surprise gone, he pushed up his sleeve. There was no way to make a bullet or knife wound look natural, but bludgeoning damage was a whole other ballgame.

I guess it's me on the wall with a baseball bat, he quipped in this real-life game of Clue. His hand hovered over the handle tattooed on his arm and his will reached beyond it into the third dimension. As he pulled the baseball bat from his body, Lokhov finally registered that his assailant was a magician and hurled his will at him, but it was too late.

In a split second, Haddock brought the bat crashing down on the triad leader's temple. When the Russian went limp, he gave him one more swing for good measure. It didn't have to kill him, just incapacitate him long enough to be tossed over the wall.

He wiped down the bat on the Russian's shirt before rejoining it with its twin inked on his arm. Then, he grabbed the triad leader's backpack, neck pouch, and phone before rolling him over the edge of the wall. There were no screams accompanying the thud as Lokhov was reunited with his team.

Haddock plugged a mini-drive into the phone and emptied the crushed velvet bag onto the stone wall-walk while the drive cloned the Russian's mobile. He gave the ring a wide berth in case it was magical or worse, cursed. However, it was as dull and lackluster as its surroundings when viewed through the hag stone.

It's not enchanted? he puzzled as he picked it up and looked it over. There was something carved in the reddish-brown stone, but he couldn't quite make it out. *What's so special about you?* he asked it as he put it back into its bag. He couldn't very well ask the dead Russians.

He pulled the night vision binoculars from the triad leader's backpack and scanned the coastline. He reasoned they must have approached by the river if they were making their exit on this side of the battlements. The incipient threads of a plan wove themselves into a neat plait as soon as he spotted the boat along the water's edge, weighted down and partially camouflaged.

Leaving the bodies where they fell was a bad idea, because they would be found sooner and their deaths would draw the authorities to the castle. Delays in their discovery and identification gave him and the Salt Mine more time to cover their tracks and figure out if this was something that warranted further intervention. Haddock threw down Stashkysnky's grappling hook and secured his own to the railing before climbing down himself. It was clean-up time.

When he reached the bottom, he verified each Russian was dead before ushering them to the coast in a series of fireman carries. Under the leafy cover, he stripped them of their phones and identification, cloning the former and taking a picture of the latter before hurling them into the river. The passports were probably fake, but they could help the analysts construct a timeline and make lateral connections. All their tactical gear went deep into the river as well: grappling hooks, binoculars, lock picks, weapons, etc.

Once all the materials were settled, he dumped the bodies into the water, pushing them out with one of the oars until the lethargic current took them. Then he removed the rocks from the boat's anti-skid deck and flipped it upside down before sending it out into the water as well. He then launched each oar into the Sûre like a javelin, and all traces of the Russians were gone.

Chapter Three

Haddock steered his rental car along the gentle curves of the dark road. He loved driving in Europe. It was a different aesthetic to North America, where grids of straight lines from point A to point B were complementary to the brutal architecture that had swept the continent in the past century. Obviously, part of it was due to geography—the Ardennes were rough terrain with rolling hills and ridges—but one couldn't discount the general European sensibility that demanded style in form and function. And although it reduced the prevalence of highway hypnosis on dynamic boulevards, he suspected it was just a perk rather than the primary, or even secondary intention.

Wallonia was the rural, French-speaking, southern portion of Belgium—a seat of industrial power dating back to the medieval ages thanks to its rich coal deposits and proximity to navigable rivers for trade. As modern European economies transitioned away from heavy industry, the region lost economic supremacy but never its sense of self.

Bastogne was quintessentially quaint. Few buildings in the city center were taller than three or four stories, all faced with brick, stone, or painted plaster. The shop displays on the ground floor were inviting while the windows of the apartments above were capped with charming awnings. During festivals, colorful streamers crossed the streets, strung from rooftop to rooftop.

It was a stark contrast to the Sherman tank parked in McAuliffe Square, one of many monuments to the U.S. 101st Airborne and their brave conduct during the Siege of Bastogne as part of the Battle of the Bulge. The town was filled with war memorabilia and museums, and it was a destination for many in and out of the military.

The steady influx of American tourists in such a rustic part of Benelux was part of the reason Haddock had picked Bastogne as a base of operation. It was only a thirty-minute drive to Schlass Wollef and he had a believable reason for spending a few days there. The same could not be said of Heiderscheidergrund, where nothing happened and the locals liked it that way.

Remaining inconspicuous was vital. After spending five years in deep cover in the Russian navy, the plan was for him to stay out of Europe for a while. Everyone that served with him on the *Yantar* had gone down with the ship, but there was still the possibility of being recognized by someone who'd known him as Petty Officer Boris Mikhailovich Petrov, or even worse, being spotted by an Ivory Tower agent who knew him as

Alex Husnik…who by all accounts died six years ago. The plan was to let enough time pass so that all the various intelligence agencies forgot about the Russian spy ship fiasco and *then* introduce him back into his favorite playground.

However, he was the perfect agent for a literary recovery mission and he'd been sent back a bit earlier than anticipated. As a scribe, he had a way with magically infused ink, even if his preferred medium was tattoos. If anyone could wrangle enchanted writings, it was him.

He circled the block until he found a parking spot and walked the cobblestoned streets to his hotel, passing empty terraces and the last of the serious late-night revelers. The smell of cigarettes and spilt beer wafted by in the cool breeze, and there was always that one loud drunk yelling defiantly at the approaching and unwanted dawn.

He snuck into the lobby behind a group of inebriated twenty-somethings. The man manning the front desk acknowledged their entrance without giving them undo scrutiny; paying customers took precedence over poor manners. Haddock peeled off the cluster and headed straight for his room, locking the door behind him.

He immediately shrugged off his pack and grabbed a bottle of sparkling mineral water. It was one of those things that was quite ordinary in Europe but utterly fancy stateside. Normally, he didn't mind the carbonation, but he hated that it got in the way of rapid rehydration. Lugging three dead Russians over his shoulder hadn't been on his agenda, and his backpack was always heavier than normal on the way back from a retrieval mission. He tore a hunk off a baguette and made a mini sandwich with the cheese and cold cuts he'd saved from earlier. While he ate, he prioritized his remaining tasks before he could get some sleep.

He started with the burgundy velvet sachet. By angling the desk lamp, he was able to take detailed pictures of the silver signet ring. When he couldn't quite capture the carving, he got creative and pressed it gently into putty that would normally be used to copy a key. To his untrained eye, it looked like a lion rampant—something found often enough in heraldry—but Chloe and Dot would know better.

He tapped out a message and marked it PRIORITY before sending the pictures to the twins. The ring would be in their hands in two days' time, but there was a chance they could identify it from the photos alone. Their breadth of their knowledge and speedy recall never ceased to amaze him. The presence of the Ivory Tower gave the ring precedence over his original mission objective, but it wasn't something that needed immediate attention, otherwise he would have marked it URGENT.

Next, he opened the plastic bag and carefully slid out its cloth-wrapped content. He recognized the fabric as conservator's silk and donned nitrile gloves before peeling back the folds. It was a slim collection of pages, held together by a central fold punctuated with small holes from where they had once been sewn together. The edges were rough but the pages uniform in size, which suggested it was a single sheet folded multiple times with the exterior seams cut rather than a collection of individually cut pieces folded in half.

As he flipped through the sixteen-paged quire, the spreads alternated in color—a contrast typical of vellum stemming from the differences in the interior and exterior aspects of the animal's skin. The lighter pages were the flesh side while the ones with a darker cast were the hair side.

The absence of a title page and the 21 at the bottom of the final page suggested it was part of a larger work. However, there were no marks on the upper right corner of each spread; older works historically favored numbering folios rather than each individual page.

The text was written in black ink in a single block from left to right, and there was no punctuation except for little stars denoting new paragraphs like medieval bulletin points. The script looked Roman, but he couldn't decipher any words despite the fact that he knew many Romantic languages.

In his experience, enchanted works *wanted* to be read and used, but this one was giving him the metaphorical cold shoulder. It seemed both familiar but completely incomprehensible, which struck him as odd given his connection with the written word, especially enchanted ones. Even as a kid, mundane words seemed to jump off the page and come to life in his brain, and the affinity grew stronger when his arcane talent bloomed.

Maybe the ink isn't magical or it's being esoterically caged? He postulated as he took pictures of each spread for the twins. As he folded the protective cloth back over the vellum, a stitched design on the bottom right-hand corner caught his eye. It was a Doric column with a flame hovering above it and the letter L beside it with its bottom line wrapped around the column's base like a ribbon.

He recognized it as the logo for Ignis Liber, an antiquarian bookstore run by one Feliks Sebek, a Bulgarian of questionable morals. The physical shop was located in Sofia, but as part of the European Union's single market, it took full advantage of free movement of goods and capital across its members' borders.

It was an ideal base from which to sell the things that reputable auction houses wouldn't touch. Sebek never pressed too hard about provenance, and it was easy to incentivize local law enforcement to look elsewhere if the need ever arose. The former Soviet Balkan nation was generally considered the most corrupt EU member country, and a little bribery and graft was all part of doing business. If there was a buyer and a seller, it was business as usual as long as Sebek got his cut. Who cares about where things came from and where they went?

Ivory Tower and Ignis Liber? What was the late graaf into? He wondered as he photographed the logo to include with the other pictures and sent them along.

Last but not least, Haddock hoisted the book safe to the

desk. It was no larger than a cigar box but weighed close to seventy pounds due to the twenty-seven titles held between its leatherbound wooden boards. In order to make it safe to hold magical works, Weber had employed arcane compression to increase the density of the books instead of using an extra dimensional space, which would have not only reduced their size but also their weight.

Haddock was dubious at first; having something that reminded him of a portable mini black hole seemed like a terrible idea, but the inventor had assured him it was perfectly safe. The compression field was caged and it only worked on books, scrolls, and codices because, well, magic.

Weber had tried to explain the finer metaphysical points—how checking for a change in mass was one of the differential tests of extra dimensional space in enchanted storage—but Haddock zoned out as soon as he got his hands on a book and saw the book safe in action. Once the tome was within a foot of the open box, the book—and only the book—progressively shrank until it could fit on the miniature shelf. When he watched it grow back to original size as he pulled it off the shelf, he was sold.

He opened the cover and looked at the rows of tiny spines—not a bad haul for a night's work considering he had been so rudely interrupted. He'd used the hag stone to quickly identify the enchanted works, which had to be confiscated even if they ended up being relatively innocuous. The much more difficult task was finding books that were not magical but contained dangerous information. Any other agent would have to systematically go through the library one book at a time, but not Haddock, which was why he was sent to Europe earlier than planned.

He could simply clear his head, cast his will wide, and browse the stacks. Although its pull was more subtle than enchanted works, arcane knowledge also beckoned to be used. He was particularly sensitive to such things, and he thought of it as his form of "Spidey sense." Like a spider on its web, all it took was a small tug on his extended will for him to pinpoint the location of something interesting and figure out if it was dangerous. Unfortunately, he'd lost hours dealing with the Russians and in the end he'd just grabbed everything that seemed "interesting" in addition to the enchanted books, instead of taking his time as he preferred.

He pulled the little books out individually using his index fingers on the top and bottom and securing them with his whole hand as they cleared the compression radius. He only kept the gloves on to protect the tomes from the oils on his hand, not because he had anything to fear from the books.

For whatever reason, he wasn't affected by enchanted works the same way others were: he was, as far has he'd discovered, immune to their dangers. Such innate talents had landed him in repository maintenance and repair for Chloe and Dot during his convalescence. Not that he minded. He'd always had a fondness for old books, even the mischievous ones. The twins attributed it to him being a scribe, but he generally found it a fool's errand to look for logic when it came to magic.

Once the book safe was empty, he began cataloguing them for the sixth floor, starting with the ones that weren't enchanted. There was a handful of books on different disciples of magic, but most of them were harmless. *Kazimeer's Illusions for Apprentices* covered the basics, *Kemetian Fire Magic* was about channeling one's inner fire outward, *The Sixteen Transformations* was about turning oneself into various animals, and *Mesmerism* which was exactly as advertised in the name. The only one that qualified as dangerous knowledge was *The Educated Caster: Necromantics*.

There were a few titles about fiends. *Salt, Sulphur, Mercury* discussed the "vital materials" in summoning and binding demons. *Thirteen of the Nameless Devils* piqued his interest. He was under the impression that all devils had true names, even the lowliest of imps, but he was no expert on the residents of Hell. The work looked to be a brief treatise on identifying those particularly slippery devils and how to control one of them with no true name.

Living Water and *Invisible Winds* were about elementals—water and air, respectively—and *Magic from Springs* was about enchanted bodies of water. Magical springs were real but rare, and they were much sought after because they worked on everyone and they required no expenditure of will as Mother Nature picked up any karmic cost. The pinnacle was the healing spring because it was one of the few times magic could actually heal injuries and illnesses, although the Fountain of Youth was a close second. The main problem with magical springs was that they lost their magic over time: one never knew when the last magic drink was about to be imbibed.

Next, he flipped through *Pentachordianism*, a pamphlet outlining tenets of a religious order of arcane ascetics who believed five musical chords held the key to the universe. It posited that playing these chords in the right order would unlock one's potential as the spirit became harmonically attuned to the universe. Of course, they didn't actually know the chords and conveniently, there was righteousness to be found just in the seeking. He imagined their services sounded something like a fusion of jazz improvisation and progressive music over a drone.

This should give Chloe and Dot a good laugh, he mused as he put it back in the book safe next to a pair of early Masonic essays: *Mathemagics* and *The Science of Circles*. He chuckled. *Just goes to show that even bunk has a desire to be read.*

With all the mundane books sorted, he started with the enchanted stuff. The first five were a collection of works about a place called Dimwash: *Dimwash Flows, Dimwash Frogs, Dimwash Herbal, Dimwash Trees, and Dimwash Water Foods.* They were enchanted, but not in a malevolent sense. The creator used simple illusions to enhance the work—a dynamic illustration of a flower opening and closing according to its diurnal rhythm, the croak of a frog with a distinct mating call, a three-dimensional rendering of a waterfall, or the texture, appearance, and smell of an herb when it's ready for harvest. It must have seemed wondrous in a time before photography, video, or sound recording, and as far as he knew, modern technology had yet to create smell-o-vision so there was still wonder to be found. *Score one for magic*, he thought as he placed them on a different shelf from the non-magical books.

There was another set: a six-volume work called *Symbolic Language*. The enchanted encyclopedia of arcane runes was designed to be a reference for practicing magicians, but as he flipped through the pages, it became clear that some of the magic had gone bad as the more powerful symbols took over and twisted the arcane power to their will rather than the intent of its creator.

He felt a grasping tug, not unlike a recalcitrant kindergartener refusing to let go of a parent at drop off. "Definitely one for the repository," he muttered under his breath as he separated the three questionable books from the others. *One bad apple can ruin the bunch* he aphorized as he put each in a plastic bag, placed that in another bag, and filled it in with salt. The remaining three books in the series were stacked next to the Dimwash set.

Next was a pair of books written by someone named Talbot. The first was a scholastic work titled *True Names*. Unlike the previous enchanted works, there wasn't anything obviously magical about it—no locks, booby traps, or fantastic sensory displays. He ran his will over it, looking for more information and found a chink: a magical core that was subtly hidden.

It screamed esoteric extra dimensional book safe and his curiosity demanded he investigate, but he backed off when he sensed how eager the magic was at the thought. If he did open it, there was no guarantee about what would be inside, how dangerous it was, or if he would be able to cram it back into the book.

I'll leave it for the twins, he told himself as he reluctantly left well enough alone. Like all librarians, they liked a good puzzle.

The second work of Talbot was untitled and jumped straight in without preface or introduction. Haddock recognized the letters but couldn't read it, either because it was magically scrambled, written in code, or both. The line between being protective of one's work and outright paranoid was easily blurred, and to be honest, a lot of practitioners tended toward the nutty on the best of days.

He'd never heard of Talbot before, but based on the prevalence of demonic symbols, necromantic runes, and detailed dissection diagrams, he surmised that Talbot was into some dark shit. Even its metaphysical touch left an oily residue that made him want to take a shower. On his inventory list, he called it *Talbot's Grimoire*—which sounded so much cooler than journal, diary, or even spellbook—before placing both of his works back on the miniature shelves.

He saved the weirdest for last. *Yonglang Star Chart* was a codex folded like a concertina and as soon as he opened it, his hotel room lit up in twinkling lights. As he moved through the codex and changed the spread, the stars shifted across the plaster. It was like sitting in a planetarium except the constellations were foreign to him and the stars were more brilliant than any he'd seen before. He closed it up and read the fine print: The Night Sky of the Outerlands in each Epoch. *Probably something for the Iron Mine's library.*

He closed the cover and locked the book safe with a twist of his will. He sent one final message to the librarians, giving them a heads up on what he was bringing in. The sky was lightening and he checked the time. It was early but no longer an ungodly hour. He sent Alicia Moncrief—codename Clover—a warning: *be on alert, Ivory Tower encountered.*

The heiress-slash-Salt Mine operative was ostensibly in town for Graaf Hendrik van der Meer's funeral, but she was supposed to rendezvous with him afterward and courier the goods back to Detroit on her metallic cobalt blue G650. Unsurprisingly, security wasn't as stringent for private jets, and she had the gear to contain willful magic.

He extended sleep mode on his phone. It had been a long night and he hoped to get some rest before meeting Moncrief. It wouldn't stop any critical messages from the Mine, but that was the nature of field work. Thankfully, his years in the navy had taught him two important skills: how to catch Zs whenever and wherever he could get them and to rouse quickly to a call for action. His vision blacked out as he pulled down a silk eye cover and he slipped quietly into slumber.

Chapter Four

Harold Weber nervously ran his wrinkled hand through his unruly white hair. It always had a mind of its own, but today, it was extra ornery. He was weeks overdo for a haircut but it kept getting pushed back. There were more pressing matters on his plate.

Delivering secure internet access to the fifth and sixth floor had been on his to-do list for a while, and it was finally happening...provided that he and colleague, Hans Lundqvist, could make it work. Weber had long considered a direct physical connection to the internet backbone, but he couldn't get the security to Leader's exacting standard until Hans arrived. After integrating magic into both the hardware and programming, they were given permission to beta test in the workshop. After adjustments were made, they then alpha tested on their own computers—magical encryption, arcane firewalls, runed cables, sigiled filters...the whole works.

Everyone celebrated when it passed muster and Leader gave them the green light to hook up the desktops. Wi-Fi for mobiles, laptops, and tablets was out of the question, but at least the agents, and librarians would no longer have to surface to access the internet and Hans could now watch his programs in his sixth-floor accommodations.

Setting up the agents' office computers had gone smoothly, but the tower in the library wasn't so accommodating. Chloe had resisted upgrading for years because "she liked this one and knew how to use it." As soon as he opened it up, he knew it was going to be a bear with the older parts. Magic was fickle and therefore a challenge to meld with technology—which could be temperamental in its own right—and this was a little more complicated than connecting to a router or network.

Hans was in the process of reassembling the motherboard with its new components when Weber neutrally asked, "*Bist du sicher?*"

The younger blond man paused to consider the question. He mentally doubled checked the circuitry, redid the math, and weighed the statistical probability against the consequence of failure. Meanwhile, Weber removed his thick glasses and carefully wiped them with a handkerchief extracted from one of the many pockets of his work apron.

"*Ziemlich sicher,*" the Swede answered honestly. "*Hast du eine bessere Idee?*"

If anyone else had asked the same question, Weber would have checked for subtext, but during their brief time working together Hans had established himself as a very literal, direct person. That and his fluency in German made the honest exchange of ideas flow smoothly between the two inventors. They were just two scientists working on a problem.

Weber held up his glasses to the light and deemed his lenses clean enough. He folded the linen square and placed it back into its pocket. "*Nein,*" the older man admitted, "*um der Wissenschaft willen.*"

Hans gave him a slight smile and nodded. "*Für den Fortschritt.*"

"Everything okay back there?" Chloe inquired from a nearby rectangular table usually reserved for visitors. She and Dot had been evicted from their typical perch behind the circular desk while the computer was being worked on. She'd let the sparks, mechanical sounds, and casting slide, but the uptick in German chatter over her partially dissembled motherboard had her worried.

"Yes, of course," Weber switched to English. "Hans is just putting everything back together and then we will turn it on and make sure everything is working," he reassured her.

"Well, okay…" Chloe assented with a perfunctory smile, but she quietly voiced her doubts to her sister. "How long does it take? They've been at it all morning."

"It would go faster if you didn't pester them," Dot pointed out. It felt strange being the advocate for patience, but she was enjoying the moral superiority in this bizarre reversal of roles.

"I want my computer back," Chloe whispered emphatically.

"When you get it back, you'll have access to the web. Isn't that worth it?" Dot said sweetly.

"If they can get it to work. Right now, it's in pieces," Chloe objected.

Having quickly exhausted her bank of comforting words, Dot grunted empathetic noises. She and Chloe had been literally joined at the hip their whole lives—Chloe on the right, Dot on the left—and she wasn't supposed to be the reasonable one. The surlier twin dug deep and came up with a classic Chloe play: deflect and distract.

"I'm sure Leader will get you a new one if they royally mess this one up. In the meantime, a watched pot never boils. Why don't you focus on work," Dot suggested in her best impersonation of her sister.

"But I don't *want* a new one," Chloe huffed and redirected her focus on her tablet. At least she was able to get their messages before they took the desktop apart. "Any information on the ring?" she asked in a renewed effort to concentrate on something other than the interlopers at their circular desk.

Dot picked up her coffee mug. "It looks like one of the van Verdun rings."

Chloe shrugged. "That makes sense. It was found in their ancestral home."

"Yes, except it was supposed to be lost to history," Dot dropped the other shoe and let the suspense build as she took a sip. "The original five van Verdun brothers created identical signet rings that were to be passed down their lineages, to represent the branches of the family that could inherit the ancestral property. As the family tree hit terminal branches, the rings returned to the estate. Hendrik van der Meer was considered the last ring bearer, with a total of four rings."

Chloe spotted the discrepancy immediately. "But there were five brothers," she interjected.

Dot nodded. "The legend is that one ring was lost during the Ottoman siege of Arkadi during the Cretan Revolt in 1866. The Eastern Orthodox monastery held out for a few days, but the Ottomans eventually broke in. In a desperate gambit, the abbot set fire to the store of gunpowder in the monastery's vaults. The subsequent explosion killed nearly a thousand people, many of which were women and children who had taken refuge there. One of those who had taken refuge was a ring bearer, and from that point forth the fate of that branch was unknown."

"And the ring was never recovered?" Chloe guessed.

In a blasé gesture, Dot shrugged her shoulders and replied, "That's what conventional lore says."

"But the Ivory Tower knew about it and was looking for it?" Chloe skeptically asked.

"Makes you wonder…." Dot agreed. "We'll know more when it arrives. What about the manuscript?"

"I don't want to be premature, but I think I've found something." Chloe tried her best to downplay the gravity of her discovery but the sparkle in her eyes undermined her attempt. Despite her protests to the contrary, she had the worst poker face.

Dot gladly returned to their standard dynamic and rolled her eyes. *Such a drama queen.* "Obviously, we will have to revise any hypothesis once we have the actual manuscript," she gave her sister the obligatory proviso of wiggle room.

"I think it's a quire of the Voynich manuscript," Chloe stated simply.

Dot almost spit out her coffee but forced herself to swallow. "*The* Voynich manuscript?" she clarified. "The untranslatable work with pictures of planetary bodies that don't resemble our solar system and plants not known on Earth…that Voynich manuscript?" Named after the Polish rare books dealer that purchased it in 1912, the Voynich manuscript's origins, authorship, and meaning were a mystery, even to the librarians.

"I know!" Chloe exclaimed. "I can't say for certain, but it's done in the same style and it's not in any language I can identify." In spite of how many languages they knew between them—living and dead—neither of them could decipher the manuscript, a fact that both of them found absolutely maddening.

"And there's a 21 on the last page of the quire," Chloe added to strengthen her case. Everyone knew there were missing pages, but the existence of an entirely new quire was groundbreaking. She zoomed in on the digits and slid the tablet to her left.

Dot put down her mug and took a good look. "If it's a fake, whoever did it did their homework. There's no 'm' or '9' after the quire number, just like in quire 19 and 20," she commented.

She oriented the image to the top right of the page and searched for numbers but found none. "And if it's genuine, it was removed before the folios were marked."

Dot scrolled through the pages of text with the swipe of her finger, looking for illustrations. The familiar but inscrutable script flew by, until suddenly, she realized that she understood some of the words.

Chloe sensed something was amiss when Dot abruptly stopped her aimless browsing. "What is it?"

Dot stared at the screen. "Chloe, I can read it."

Chloe laughed and nudged her sister's side. "Good one. You almost had me for a second."

"No, I'm serious," Dot stood firm, and Chloe didn't even try to hide her disbelief.

To prove her point, Dot started at the first star on the electronic page. "Carefully remove five seeds from a biting flower…dry it for a full moon cycle…crush into a fine powder…add to the syrup of a milky pine under a low flame… if the smoke turns bitter—no, acrid—it is ruined."

It had taken her some time to work through the line, but once she said it out loud, she knew exactly what it meant, like someone who was fluent in a language but illiterate and learning to read. "It's a recipe," she said triumphantly with her pert nose upturned.

Chloe took the tablet in hand and took a harder look at the script—*nothing*. "Okay, say you are reading it," she played along. "What language is it in?"

A vague look came over Dot's face. "I have no idea. I don't recognize it as language I know, but I understand it."

"Try reading it out loud as written. Maybe I'll recognize it aurally," Chloe offered in an attempt to be helpful.

"That's what I'm trying to tell you, Chloe! I'm not translating it from anything. I just know it."

Something in Dot's frustration struck her as genuine. "You're not kidding." Dot threw up her hands to pantomime equal parts *finally* and a sarcastic *thank you.* "Maybe it's a fake using fae sigils?" Chloe grasped at straws.

"And I'm the intended audience and not you?" Dot asked incredulously. "Unlikely."

Chloe chewed on her bottom lip and thought out loud. "We can't study its arcane composition until it gets here but see if you can read established parts of the manuscript."

Dot closed her blue eyes and walked her memory palace until she reached the Voynich room. She recalled f66r amongst the herbal section, which included one of her favorite bit of marginalia. Someone had drawn a naked man on the bottom left corner and wrote "*der Mussteil*" next to it. She understood the High German—a widow's share—but the rest of the words drew a blank. "Nope," she sighed. Her disappointment was palpable.

"When's the last time you looked at the original?"

"Years...maybe decades?" Dot wagered a guess. Time was a nebulous construct when one was as old as the twins.

"Maybe you just need to see the real thing and not your memory of it," Chloe suggested. While robust, their memory wasn't infallible, no matter what they might say to others.

"I've got nothing else better to do," Dot drily replied.

The librarians stood up and the sound of the chairs pushing away from the table startled Weber and Hans. "We'll be right back. Just need to find something in the stacks. Keep working!" Chloe gently pressed them to stay on task.

The twins moved in unison, weaving through the rows of bookshelves. They knew the library like the back of their hand, and it wasn't just because they had eidetic memories. They had carved it out of the salt and created a system for cataloging enchanted writing and works about magic from the ground up. Magic might have eluded rational logic, but it couldn't avoid being categorized by the discerning mind of a true librarian, much less two.

While the world regarded the goatskin-wrapped collection housed in the Beinecke Rare Book and Manuscript Library at Yale University as the Voynich manuscript, it was actually a reproduction. Chloe and Dot had recreated it using period materials and methods with a dash of magic. It was arguably some of their best work, indistinguishable from the original. It had even withstood a gauntlet of modern tests, including carbon dating, polarized light microscopy, energy-dispersive X-ray spectroscopy, X-ray diffraction, and scanning electron microscopy.

The original was, in fact, in the Salt Mine. There had been much debate on where to store it. It was definitely enchanted, but no one could say for what purpose or effect. It was just another way in which it was enigmatic—usually magic wanted to be used, but the Voynich manuscript came off as esoterically inert upon examination. It eventually came to rest in the stacks; the repository was reserved for dangerous magical books, and it hadn't done anything that suggested it was an artifact that warranted isolated storage deeper in the Mine.

The librarians hastily donned gloves before they ushered the manuscript to a lectern for support. Enchanted or not, preservation was key. Dot opened to folio sixty-six. The left-hand side had a prominent illustration of a plant from roots to flowers. The smaller blooms had large centers encircled by a short fringe, like a sunflower with stunted petals. Rising above them was an elongated blue trumpet flower.

Dot used her index finger as a guide as she started reading the rechto side, or the right-hand page in layman's terms. "The Lapis Bolt gets its name from the brilliant blue flower that blooms from its dominant stalk as it goes to seed. When the petals open at night, it releases a sweet fragrance to attract pollinators.

"This can be used in perfume making if harvested at night and its essence distilled in spirits. Beware of its thistles.

"The faux seeds of the smaller white blossoms can be harvested and ground into dust which certain fairies prize as a narcotic."

As Dot stumbled slowly through the paragraphs, Chloe tried to wrap her mind around what she was witnessing. The Voynich manuscript had eluded comprehension for centuries and here her sister was, reading it.

"What's this caption say?" Chloe quizzed her, pointing to the writing around the base of the illustration on f65v.

Dot turned her attention to the opposite page and focused. "The Lapis Bolt favors loamy soil with at least partial sun and temperate temperatures. It is often found along forest floors for those foraging wild variants. Easy to domesticate, but its root system is aggressive. Plant in a pot or separate enclosure to control growth." Dot looked up and grinned wide. It was mentally taxing, but she could read it. So pure was her joy, there was no trace of sarcasm or nihilism behind the smile.

"It doesn't make sense," Chloe objected as she closed the book. Dot eked out a squeak but voiced no other objection when she saw her sister's expression. She called it Chloe's *Oh-hell-no! face.* "I think we should have you checked out before you do any more reading."

Dot sighed. "That's probably not a bad idea."

Chloe immediately became suspicious. Dot wasn't known for being agreeable. "What aren't you telling me?"

"I don't want you to freak out," Dot prefaced, "but I now have two memories of this folio: one that I understand, and one that I don't."

"And they are both stored in the same place?" Chloe alluded to the memory palace.

Dot nodded. "Like saving a file without overwriting the old one."

Chloe slipped the Voynich manuscript back on the shelf. "That settles it, then. We're going to the fourth floor."

Chapter Five

Sofia, Bulgaria
4th of September, 3:30 p.m. (GMT+2)

Within forty-eight hours, Haddock had undergone a transformation. He had a fresh haircut and a clean shave, and Moncrief had dressed him to the nines before flying the items taken from Schlass Wollef back to the Mine. He'd traded his t-shirt and jeans for an Armani suit and silk tie, and his chestnut Gucci lace-up leather loafers were polished to a shine. Instead of a backpack, he carried an attaché along with his standard-issue Salt Mine luggage. He even changed his ink, trading the Louisville Sluggers for a crossed pair of cricket bats. He was no longer Aaron Haddock, American tourist visiting WWII sites in Benelux, but Adam Hargrove, British entrepreneur that specialized in imports and exports.

Hargrove was one of the few aliases that survived Alex Husnik's untimely death, largely because the Mine was certain that the Ivory Tower had never made the connection that the two were the same. While he was serving in the Russian navy, the Mine kept his British alias alive through remote transactions and communications. All the major auction houses knew the name, even if they hadn't seen the man himself.

It was a calculated risk to physically revive Hargrove so close to Russian territory, but he'd argued there was no time like the present. The bodies he'd dumped in the Sûre River hadn't been reported to the authorities and Moncrief didn't catch a whiff of Ivory Tower or SVR at the funeral. If he acted fast, he would be in and out of Bulgaria before anyone knew the wiser even if someone was looking for him, which there shouldn't be. He'd eluded unwanted detection for years and had every faith he could do so again.

It didn't take him long to resurrect Hargrove from his internal cast of characters. He liked nice things, which was why LaSalle booked him first-class travel and five-star luxury accommodations. He preferred gin martinis and had an even drier sense of humor. His appreciation for beauty was only matched by his eye for value. And when it came to business, he was bent as a dog's hind leg.

When his car pulled up to the front entrance of the Grand Hotel Sofia, he waited for the driver to get the door before walking down the red carpet. His stride wasn't as bold or base as a swagger or strut, but there was an undeniable confidence that the discerning would interpret as the vestigial pride of imperial days past. The sound of his hard-soled shoes on the champagne and brown marble floors of the foyer echoed against the marble until he stopped at the front desk.

When the receptionist turned her large brown eyes from

the computer screen, she gave him a warm smile. She was accustomed to businessmen in nice suits, but it was nice to see one that was handsome, fit, and not old for a change. "Good afternoon. How may I help you?"

He returned the grin as he slid his ID over the smooth counter. "I'd like to check in. Adam Hargrove." While her fingers tapped over the keyboard, he ran his eyes over her, subtle enough to avoid coming off as creepy but overt enough to be a compliment if she so wanted it to be. Hargrove was a shameless flirt. Haddock liked Hargrove.

She felt his eyes on her as she performed a series of well-practiced movements: click the mouse, swipe the keycard, slip in an insert in the cardboard jacket, and write in the room number. She brushed off his gaze with a flick of her auburn curls over her shoulder before presenting him the packet.

"Welcome to the Grand Hotel Sofia, Mr. Hargrove. We've been expecting you. Your room is ready." She slid his check-in folder across the counter and used her red-polished fingernail to point out his room number. "Would you like some help with your luggage?"

"That won't be necessary. Where are the lifts?"

"Down that hall." She motioned with her hand and politely dismissed him. He took the brush off with aplomb; Hargrove may be a bit of a rogue with the ladies, but he was always a gentlemanly one. He followed her instructions and then he rode the elevator to his floor where he followed the overtly decorative signs to his room.

He did a cursory walk-through and appraised his accommodations. It was clean, airy, and stylish. The bed was firm like he liked it with plenty of pillows. There was no need to check for cameras or bugs because he was method. He wouldn't break character until he was out of Bulgaria. Anyone monitoring the room would see and hear exactly what he wanted them to: a foreign business traveler in town for work.

However, he did put a minor apathy ward on his luggage. It would be enough to keep out a nosy housekeeper, but more importantly, it would let him know if someone more determined had searched his things. Not that there was anything to find—anything sensitive was on his person at all times.

He phoned reception for a dinner reservation and for housekeeping to send up more towels. He gave them high marks for their turnaround time, and when the clock ticked over to the other side of half past four, Hargrove left his room with his attaché and strolled onto the pleasantly warm streets of Sofia.

Sofia had been continuous settled since the fifth century BCE and was influential during Roman times, but it was little more than a small town when Bulgaria gained its independence from the Ottoman Empire in 1878. The spirit of the times demanded more from the nation's new capital, and the city became a planned urban space modeled after the two progressive darlings of the day, Paris and Vienna.

Laid out in a radial-circled pattern, its wide boulevards were lined with grand buildings in the style of the Viennese Secession—an aesthetic movement related to but distinctly different from Art Nouveau. Many of them were destroyed during the war and replaced with edifices of socialist realism. After the fall of the Eastern Bloc, Bulgaria reinvented itself again and Sofia modernized in a post-Soviet world.

The end result was a patchwork of cultures, faiths, and times standing side-by-side on a small piece of real estate. Within a short walk from his hotel was the oldest public garden, an amphitheater built over the remains of a Roman one, the largest Orthodox Church in the country built to commemorate independence from the Ottomans, early Christian churches built in the fourth and sixth centuries, the largest synagogue in the Balkans, and a sixteenth century mosque. The grand theaters and museums ranged from pre-war, between the wars, post-war, and post-Soviet. And of course, there was a McDonald's.

But Hargrove wasn't there to sightsee. His destination was an old storefront that had refused to renovate or sell. The sign out front was the same—Ignis Liber, inspired by the Promethean myth and the notion that books were the flame of knowledge through which humanity could lift itself to loftier states. He sent his will ahead of him, getting the esoteric lay of the land as he approached the thick wooden front door. It was battered and worn, but the delicate curves of the carved repeating geometric pattern with floral motifs were still visible.

It squeaked on its sturdy hinges as he entered—Sebek's low-tech version of a doorbell. A familiar face popped out from behind a bookcase at the sound of the door opening. His hair was thinner and a lighter shade of brown, fading on its way to gray, but there was no doubt in his mind that it was Sebek. The two men made eye contact and the Bulgarian's brown eyes lit up when he recognized Hargrove.

"Welcome to my store," he said in accented English with a calm that belied his obvious excitement. "We'll be closing at five, but please feel free to look around." Hargrove read between the lines and nodded to show he understood the subtext: they were not alone.

Sebek returned to his customer, a woman looking for a gift for her father who was a consummate bibliophile. The book dealer switched to Russian and resumed their conversation. She explained how difficult it was to shop for her father, but she'd brought a list of books he already owned in hopes that would help someone experienced in such matters find something suitable.

Haddock sent out his metaphysical feelers while he played the part of Hargrove. Shops like Ignis Liber were a dying breed; who knew what gems were hidden away in a place like this? The collective aroma of all those old books and their previous owners constituted its own signature scent, and there was nary a sign to guide the casual browser. The stuffed shelves and towers of stacked spines felt like they wanted to acquire a respectable patina of dust if only the shopkeeper would stop spoiling the affair with his ever-present duster. The books weren't placed in alphabetical order or by topic.

He had no doubt there was a system of which titles went where, but it was a mystery to all but Sebek, who worked hard to ensure that he was the fastest route to finding a sought-after work. When someone did find something on their own, the serendipity triggered a rush of dopamine that was more akin to an archeologist finding something on a dig. It elevated the book to the status of a prized treasure, which increased the chance of it being purchased.

While other bookstores tried to make their shops an experience, there were no such frills and extras here. There was no coffee nook or comfy oversized chairs to encourage lingering—if someone wanted to read a book, they should buy it and take it home. Ignis Liber wasn't a library.

Haddock's nostalgic streak was pleased to see the store hadn't changed much since last he saw it. It was genuine in its worn and rough spots, a departure from the manufactured trajectory retail had taken. There wasn't anything "McDonald's" about Sebek's bookstore except that you could see one across the square when looking out the front window. As he waited for Sebek to finish, Haddock picked out a few books that he wouldn't mind purchasing as he thought it was a good idea to buy at least a little from the shop on every visit.

Once Sebek had found an ideal book that just happened to be on the upper end of her budget, he led his customer to the counter against the back wall. He rang up the transaction and while she paid, Sebek wrapped the book up with care. He was a man that took pride in his work, clutter aside.

They exchanged pleasantries on their way to the door, which he closed and locked behind her. Sebek flipped the sign in the window to "closed" before addressing Haddock.

"Adam, long time, no see!" the bear of a man roared jovially. Sebek was average height but built like an ox. "Where have you been hiding all this time?"

"Abroad. Europe was getting crowded," Hargrove replied curtly as they shook hands.

Sebek accepted the vague explanation. Many of his associates had cause at one time or another to get out of town and lie low. "I see you've found some things," he changed the subject when he spied the short stack of books in Haddock's other hand.

"I always find something interesting in your store, Feliks," Haddock greased the wheels with a little flattery. He placed the books on the counter next to the credit card machine by the antique cash register. The modern electronic seemed out of place, but Sebek was never one to make it harder to get paid. "But these aren't why I came. I'm in the market for a buyer."

"And you come to me?" Sebek affected modesty. "You flatter me, Adam. But surely you have extensive contacts."

"I had one lined up, but it fell through at the last minute," Haddock replied to Sebek's oblique request for more information. "I believe my original buyer had worked with you before. I thought perhaps you might have a ready pool of customers interested in work of a similar vein, perhaps someone that was outbid in the past."

Sebek raised a bushy eyebrow. "Are you looking for an expedited sale?"

"I'm not in a rush," he insisted, "but I would like to recoup my investment sooner rather than later."

The British and their distaste of talking about something as crude as money, Sebek thought as he nodded and took a seat on the high-backed stool behind the counter. This perch placed the average man a little higher than most customers, a position he preferred when fielding questions and orchestrating deals. "Tell me, what are you selling?"

Haddock opened his attaché and produced a handful of pictures of fake Voynich material Dot had whipped up at the last minute to lure in Sebek. They didn't have to stand up to rigorous verification—one of the Salt Mine's shadow buyers would be the highest bidder—but it had to look good enough to get the Bulgarian to bite and Hargrove's reputation lent it an air of credibility.

Sebek recognized it immediately as Voynich in style and cursed in Bulgarian under his breath. "It always comes in threes." He was an open-minded man that acknowledged everyone had their thing, but even he found the Voynich connoisseurs a nutty lot, little more than conspiracy theorists with too much time and/or wealth. The only reason Sebek dealt with them at all was because of how easy it was to part them from their money.

"Come again?" Haddock feigned ignorance. Even though he knew Bulgarian, Hargrove did not.

Sebek switched back to English and waved a dismissive hand. "Nothing, just talking to myself." He made a show of examining each picture before coolly replying, "I may know someone who would be interested in this."

"It better not be Hendrik van der Meer," Haddock said bitterly and watched Sebek's face for his reaction.

"What is the world coming to?" Sebek asked rhetorically and added a derisive pftt. "In my day, when a man made an arrangement, he honored it, much less a graaf."

"To be fair, he didn't back out. He died," Hargrove replied drily.

Sebek seemed genuinely surprised at the news. "When?"

"Last week. Car accident in the Swiss Alps, I believe."

"Ah, that's unfortunate," Sebek lamented but in his head, he was already forecasting future profits based on his cut—which went up on an expedited sale—and the prospective price of the item. "But he is not the only one interested in such things. How much are you looking for?"

Haddock slipped a folded piece of paper across the counter.

Inside was a substantial figure written in blue ink. Sebek didn't fail to notice it was written on a notepad from the Grand Hotel Sofia. Below it, he penned another number: his take. He refolded the paper and passed it back.

Haddock pursed his lips at the digits. "How quickly can you move it?"

Sebek shrugged. "Maybe a week. I'll drop five percent if I can't arrange something by then," he offered, which only meant he already had a couple of buyers in mind. Haddock smiled on the inside. There was something honest about how crooked Sebek was.

"I have no objection to everyone getting paid, but I like to know who I'm dealing with," he stated his condition upfront. Sebek made a non-committal gesture that indicated this would not be a problem. He was willing to bend the rules of confidentiality for such a price.

Haddock tucked the paper into his jacket pocket. "Your terms are acceptable."

A broad smile broke out on Sebek's face. "Before we talk details, we should have a drink," he insisted as he pulled two glasses and a bottle of rakia from under the counter. "It is bad luck to embark on a new business deal without one."

Haddock checked his watch while the Bulgarian poured generously. He liked Feliks, but Hargrove was a snob beneath the veneer of mild-mannered politeness. "Just one," he pantomimed reluctance.

Sebek cheerfully clapped him on the back and handed him a glass. "*Nazdrave!*"

He sniffed the fragrant fruit brandy suspiciously before clinking his glass to Sebek's. "Cheers."

Sebek downed his rakia and grinned at he looked at the short stack of books Haddock had selected. "Now, about these books…"

Chapter Six

Detroit, Michigan, USA
5th of September, 3:30 p.m. (GMT-4

Chloe typed away on her keyboard, grateful that her computer was back in one piece and working faster than before. It wasn't unusual for the librarians to work nights and weekends when there were agents in the field, but the workload had rested more heavily on her shoulders the past few days. Most of Dot's time had been spent on all things Voynich.

Chloe looked at the time on the screen. Leader had recommended Dot limit the duration and frequency of her sessions translating the manuscript. *Fifteen more minutes*, she mentally noted before continuing her work.

When both LaSalle and Leader had declared Dot sound and fundamentally unchanged, it was reassuring but also confounding. Chloe obviously didn't want anything to be wrong with Dot, but she'd hoped for some explanation for her newfound abilities. Through supervised trial and error, Dot figured out how to read the Voynich manuscript faster than the snail's crawl she'd been struggling at without making a duplicate memory—mind meld with it.

It was a form of telepathic connection that wasn't language dependent, a skill that Dot—but not Chloe—could do. It wasn't something she did lightly, but when it was called for,

Dot could really understand the nature of a person or thing. It was part of the reason she was so gruff and Chloe took care of the niceties for the two of them—Chloe had the luxury of being able to imagine things were better than they were. Dot knew better.

In order for Dot to telepathically communicate with the magic of the Voynich manuscript, she had to go to their null space, a metaphysical location the sisters shared—like twin language, only spatially. Chloe had accompanied her the first few times to make sure it was safe, but it was as exciting as watching paint dry. Once she was fairly certain the risks were low, Dot started going by herself while Chloe cleared their workload in the physical world. They had always played to their individual strengths, and this situation was no exception.

Chloe didn't mind the shift in the division of labor, but she didn't care for spending so much time by herself. It wasn't uncommon for one of them to retreat into the null space to cool down whenever they'd had a blowout fight, but such stints were usually brief. They were born two souls in one body and inertia always pulled them back together. She couldn't blame Dot for being enthusiastic at such an opportunity, but it felt wrong being without her for so much time.

Technically, Dot was sitting right next to her, but it was just her physical shell. Her consciousness was elsewhere. At first, it was nice to work without distraction, but after a while, the subterranean space seemed too quiet without Dot's grumbles, non sequiturs, or snide asides and entirely too still without her fidgeting and eye rolls. While Dot was in the null space, Chloe was truly alone: a yin without her yang, a celestial body adrift without the gravity of its counterweight. She'd resorted to watching cat videos during her breaks to fight the isolation.

As the time neared, Chloe wrapped up loose ends and got bottles of water and snacks ready for Dot's return. Things like hunger and thirst had no meaning in the null space, but her physical body hadn't eaten or drank in hours.

She mentally prepared herself for resistance. Sometimes, getting Dot to leave was like prying a kid from a candy store. Chloe chalked it up to the thrill of discovery coupled with dodging routine work, but she was supposed to call LaSalle if she saw or felt any hint of change in Dot. She stretched her neck and rolled her shoulders before evening her breath and closing her eyes. After a few seconds, Chloe entered the space than only she and her sister could freely access.

The null space was a blank slate but could take on whatever window dressing they desired. At the moment, Dot had fashioned it into a dimly lit lounge with an comfy chair sized just for her. The twins had separate bodies here, and it was nice to have a seat completely to herself even if it was only metaphysically. Chloe immediately ran her will over her sister, whose combat boots were unapologetically on the furniture.

"I'm still me," Dot sardonically greeted her without looking up from her reading. The prop wasn't necessary because she was actually accessing her memory of the Voynich manuscript, but she liked the physicality of books—feeling its weight in her lap, breathing in its musty smell, and the tactile sensation of turning the pages.

After Chloe found her sister true to her word, she changed her outfit with a snap of will. She opted for a cornflower blue fit-and-flare dress with matching kitten heels and a wide-brimmed hat. The swish of a skirt made for one brushed against her bare legs as she approached Dot.

"You know I still have to check," Chloe replied sweetly. She'd spent a lifetime as her sister's keeper and her anchor to reality. Dot was a dreamer and Chloe didn't want to lose sight of her as she proverbially chased butterflies. She created a chair next to her sister out of thin air and took a seat, crossing her right leg over the left—something she couldn't normally do without kicking Dot. "Did you make progress?"

"Some," Dot said as she shut the book, signaling she wasn't going to put up a fight this time. "I think I've figured out part of the magic. There is a telepathic component built into the script, which is why it bears all the hallmarks of language but is unreadable to anyone who isn't in tune with it."

Chloe nodded thoughtfully. "That certainly explains why mind melding with it works so well, but you've always been able to do that. Why is the Voynich manuscript willing to let you read it now?"

Dot's face lit up. "I have a working theory. Remember the

outsider that killed Janice and almost consumed the world again?"

"Of course," Chloe remarked without commenting on her tactlessness. Dot may not have cared for Janice, but she was Chloe's friend and it had only been a year since the outsider known to the Sumerians as the Hollow rediscovered the mortal realm.

Dot opened the book to a folio in the astrology section and expanded a foldout. "That's where it lives," she said, pointing to the space between two spheres.

Shivers ran down Chloe's spine at the memory of the acrid, fishy stink of the Hollow's rotting appendage as it burned in the ceremonial fire and the cold inky depths of its native plane. "Are you sure?"

"Absolutely," Dot said emphatically.

"You weren't connected very long or deeply," Chloe remarked. She couldn't mind meld, but she knew there were levels of engagement. Dot had merely dipped her toes in the water, not jumped into the deep end.

Dot shrugged. "True, but it was enough to pinpoint its location and establish a portal. Who's to say it didn't send something back?"

"But Leader and LaSalle didn't find anything," Chloe countered.

"Maybe it didn't change me," Dot speculated. "Maybe it gave me something."

"Like an arcane key to unlock the Voynich script," Chloe completed the thought. "Do you think that was what Janice was trying to do when she was killed?"

Dot suddenly registered Chloe's distress and softened her tone. "I'm not sure, but it's possible. For all the kooky things Janice believed in, she was never one to back down from a challenge." Dot's attempt to say something nice got away from her but Chloe gave her credit for trying.

"I've finished cataloguing everything taken from Schlass Wollef, but Haddock sent us more pictures," Chloe brought her sister up to speed on what was happening outside of the null space.

"Doesn't he know it's Saturday?" Dot sharply remarked. "What does fish boy want now?"

"He got his hands on photos of things sold as Voynich by his contact. I threw out the obvious fakes, but there are a handful that might be genuine. I figured you could see if there is anything worth following up on. Are you ready to go?" she asked innocently.

Dot noticed Chloe didn't correct her about Stigma's latest alias and suspiciously looked at her sister straight on. It wasn't a vantage she saw often being perpetually attached to her left side, and reflections in the mirror were hardly the same. Chloe smiled and averted direct eye contact, sending her gaze down as she smoothed the folds of her skirt.

"You missed me," Dot taunted her.

"I didn't miss you. I'm accustomed to you. There's a difference," Chloe parried.

"Semantic at best," Dot reflexively jabbed, and the exchange reminded her how nice it was to have a sparring partner again. *Maybe I have been spending too much time by myself in the null space...*

Chloe readied herself for Dot's merciless barrage but the surly blonde zigged instead of zagged. The book in her lap disappeared, and she rose, combat boots planted on the non-floor. "I guess it's time to go back to the real world." She sighed and held out her right hand.

Chloe accepted the consolatory gesture, and they left the null space together. As they oriented themselves back into their physical body, the metaphysical space closed behind them, waiting for when it was next needed.

Chloe logged back into the computer while Dot made quick work of the first bottle of water before tearing open a bag of chips. Chloe tilted the screen and clicked through photos to keep Dot's greasy fingers off the mouse.

"Bunk...bunk...bunk," she passed judgment like the Queen of Hearts between rounds of croquet. "Nice illustration. Still bunk."

Dot stopped chewing when Chloe brought up the last picture. "What's this?"

Chloe pulled up the message Haddock had included. "An opened letterlock done in the Voynich style, sold two months ago."

Letterlocking was a method of securing written messages using folds and cuts, found in Europe as early as the thirteenth century. The most basic application allowed a letter to be sent without need of an envelope or outer casing, but it was also used to make communications tamper resistant. With slits, tabs, and holes placed directly into an intricately folded letter, reading other people's mail was much more complicated than steaming open an envelope and it was nigh impossible to hide the fact that it had been opened before being delivered to its intended recipient. Some letterlocks were so complex they would fall apart if they were opened incorrectly.

The multiple creases and small slits across the flattened page were consistent with a letterlock, but Dot had a few problems with that supposition. First, it was clearly vellum or parchment based on the darker coloration of the hair side, and paper was more common among letterlocks because it was substantially cheaper than animal skin pages. The number and angle of creases suggested a complicated fold, but there was no broken wax or adhesive stain to indicate it had been sealed with a fastener. And last, once a letter was unlocked, it should be legible but this was gobbledygook, albeit in the Voynich script. Even the ornamental flourishes—which were odd to include in a letter in the first place—were off. *Obviously, it could just be another fake*, she thought, *but something about it looks right.*

Dot resumed her chewing as she tried to put her finger on

it. "Could you do your thing on the computer and print me a model of it?" Despite her consummate love of memes, she never felt moved to dabble in Photoshop.

Chloe nodded and moved the screen back before rotating and resizing the images through a series of clicks. Dot poured the crumbs from the bottom of the bag into her mouth and started on the cookies.

"Do you need it in color?" Chloe asked.

"Is there a need to be being stingy with ink?" Dot mumbled sarcastically through her fourth cookie.

Chloe took her meaning and checked all the cells again before clicking print. After she'd made sure the printer had done the double-siding correctly, she placed the still-warm page to her left. "It's all yours."

Dot wiped her fingers on her skirt before handling the paper. First, she established the creases in both directions. As she rummaged through her drawers for an X-Acto knife and awl, Chloe placed a cutting mat on the circular desk to protect the wood. Dot copied the slits and holes apparent from the shadows in the pictures. Then, she started folding.

Chloe silently watched as Dot manipulated the paper in three dimensions, and there was a lot of cursing as she tried different variations without making any new creases. It was like solving a fragile Rubik's cube with no proscribed planes of movement or colored stickers to help. With each fold-in, different letters lined up to form new words and arcs become circles and scrolls.

When the page was transformed into something that resembled a belt buckle, Dot triumphantly placed it in front of her sister. "Tada!"

Chloe picked it up and examined it from all sides. There was a slight arc to it with a pair of slits running through its girth and writing along either edge. "What's that say?"

"'Follow the path and do not stray.'" Dot translated.

Chloe handed it back. "What path?"

Dot shrugged. "Let's get fish boy on it and find out."

Chloe turned back to the computer. "Okay, I'll send Haddock a message."

"After you do that, how about we call it day?" Dot suggested.

"You don't want to read more?" a surprised Chloe asked.

Dot gestured indifferently. "I could use some real food and a brainless movie before I go back in. And if I want to get another stint in before bed, I'm pretty sure it would be more comfortable for both of us at home."

Chloe typed out a fast reply and hit send. "You won't get any arguments from me."

Chapter Seven

Moscow, Russia
7th of September, 8:43 a.m. (GMT+3)

Captain Mikhail Timofeiovich Konev strode through the turquoise and mint green halls of the subbasement levels of the Lubyanka Building. The colors were chosen decades ago because they were supposed to keep people relaxed and focused. Personally, he found the palate odious; they were a garish relic of the nationalistic failures of the past. In spite of that, he also relished the sight because it meant he was one of the elite few who tread these halls and there was something attractive in that.

The Lubyanka Building was originally built for an insurance company, but the Bolsheviks seized it in 1918 and turned it into the headquarters for their secret police, the Checka. Additions were made in 1947 that doubled its size, including a windowless, top level dedicated to detaining political prisoners. It was remodeled again in 1983, but alterations to its exterior aesthetic didn't change the heart and nature of the building. It was the center of the KGB until the fall of the Soviets and was currently a substation of the FSB, headquartered across the street.

During the 1947 expansion, secret underground levels were added to accommodate the Ivory Tower—officially known as the 13th Main Directorate (Magical Surveillance) but never named in any official lists or reports. During the cold war, it was subordinate to the KGB but maintained a degree of self-determination due to the nature of its toolset. Knowing magic was real wasn't enough to govern how it could be applied to solve problems. After the dissolution of the USSR, the Ivory Tower achieved full independence as the various instruments of the state transitioned to a post-Soviet world.

The young captain's tall, fit form was weighed down by the gravitas of the building and its imposing history. It was not a place that tolerated failure and he was not a man accustomed to it. But there was no other way to interpret the sudden summons to Chairman Vladimir Volsky's office. Lieutenant Lokhov still hadn't checked in from his Luxembourg mission and the entire triad had dropped off the grid without a word.

Konev's annoyance grew with each precise click of his polished boots against the unforgiving floor, and others in the hallway gave him a wide berth as he barreled through. *How did a silver-platter mission Go pear-shaped?* he wondered. *I should have Gone in person!* he chastised himself. His frustration turned to anger as he remembered that it was Volsky's words that guided his decision to delegate on this one. If Konev was to further his position, he had to move beyond fieldwork.

Agents on the ground were tools others used to achieve results, and if he ever wanted to rise in command positions, he needed to show that he was more than a pawn. So, he'd taken Volsky's advice and now the smell of failure that followed in his wake was as thick as the plumes of incense in Saint Basil's Cathedral.

Konev clinched his jaw as his resentment swelled, which only made him angrier. Now was not the time to let his emotions get the better of him. He needed to be clear-headed before he got to the chairman's office. He counted his steps as he tamped down his rage. When he regained control, he focused his mind to the SVR mission that had gone wrong.

The plan had been simple: prop up a fake heir and bestow upon him a fake ring matching the other four rings so that the SVR could acquire a malleable puppet noble and by proxy, use of the van Verdun fortune to launder dirty money and mask shady deals. In addition to the ring, the SVR had fabricated and inserted doctored historical documentation throughout the governments of six different countries. Sometime after the funeral but before the settling of the estate, the heir would come forth displaying the ring and provide his carefully cultivated backstory. The claim would be enough to stop Luxembourg from seizing the assets, and all the planted information laid a trail of breadcrumbs to the false heir being legitimate. Unfortunately, the myth of the missing fifth ring upon which the entire ruse hinged was a lie—a secret revealed to the SVR only after they had thoroughly interrogated the elderly manservant of the sterile heir to the van Verdun estate they had just murdered.

The saving grace was that the real fifth ring was unlikely to be found, especially considering the manservant, his wife, and their children were no longer among the living. Because the graaf was a known magician, the Ivory Tower was recruited to find the ring and salvage the mission by producing a fake heir with the real fifth ring. It could be viewed as a step up from their original plan, and it allowed them to turn a failure in intelligence into an operational success.

Konev paused in front of the broad wooden doors to the chairman's domain. They seemed more imposing than normal, but he pushed through his hesitation. He was five minutes early and the alternative was stewing in his own thoughts in the hall. When he entered, the chairman's assistant eschewed the traditional pleasantries and she curtly told him he could go in. He took it as a bad sign. Volsky was waiting for him and she didn't want Konev's fortunes to rub off on her. *As if failure is contagious.*

He straightened his jacket with a sharp tug and took one final deep breath. Whatever was on the other side of the door, he would meet it head-on. He rapped a perfunctory knock before opening the door.

Konev was surprised to find that Volsky was not alone. The chairman of the Ivory Tower was sitting side-by-side another man at the long, thin conference table that occupied one side of his extensive office. The unexpected man was of average height and build with an unremarkable face framed by short dull brown hair. Despite his overwhelming banality, Konev recognized him immediately.

"Ah, Captain Konev," Volsky greeted him without a hint of his normal congeniality. "Punctual as ever. This is SVR Director Timchenko. Please, close the door and join us."

Konev complied and gulped down his dread during the brief moment his back was turned to them. Neither men rose and Konev did not take a seat.

"We have been discussing our latest shared difficulty," Volsky explained. The chairman's portly, fresh-shaven face betrayed nothing but the cigarette haze was an indication that all was not well. Volsky tended to chain-smoke when worried. Konev nodded but said nothing. It was a speak-when-spoken to meeting.

"Captain Konev," Timchenko addressed him. His voice was soft—almost hesitant—and as nondescript as his appearance. "Have you tried the Peking Duck at the new restaurant that just opened across the square?"

Konev didn't see what Chinese food had to do with anything but answered directly nonetheless. "I have not as yet, Director."

"I see," Timchenko responded, as if the captain's answer had revealed the length and breadth of the younger officer that stood before him. Timchenko spoke to Volsky, but continued looking at Konev, "So this is the man entrusted with the mission?"

"He is one of the finest. Our future," Volsky vouched. Konev unconsciously puffed his chest under the chairman's praise.

"Yes, I have read his file." Timchenko's head turned slightly to the side. "Ah, but what is known is known, and what is unknown is unknown," he stated with a small shrug. It sounded like a brainless aphorism to Konev, but Volsky's corroborative triple nod led him to believe he was missing something.

"And what is the mission status?" Timchenko continued.

"Still no report from the triad after the initial confirmation of success," Konev answered succinctly.

Timchenko raised his eyebrows while looking down. "So the news has not reached you yet. Three bodies were pulled from the Sûre River two hours ago."

Konev stood firm despite the news. "Are they ours?"

"Unconfirmed," Timchenko answered. "But they were found with an inflatable boat, so the probability is high."

Konev understood why the director was so parsimonious with the facts—one did not get to Timchenko's position without wielding the power that came with controlling the dissemination of information—but he found it irritating nonetheless.

"Possessions?" the captain asked in shorthand and silently said a prayer. *Please say they didn't find the manuscript.... If it* had been discovered, he would have to relinquish it to the Ivory Tower instead of keeping it for himself.

"The bodies had only their clothes," Volsky stated. "No identification, phones, or gear." Konev read between the lines—the signet ring had not been found with the bodies.

"It is quite the unexpected turn of events for something I was assured was direct and straightforward for people with the right…abilities," Timchenko said carefully. "What could take out three of your operatives, Captain? Even if one was green, fresh from your new training facility?"

Konev barely kept his cool in the face of such a challenge. The SVR had no jurisdiction over him; why was its director privy to internal Ivory Tower command decisions? *So much for complete operational independence.* He bitterly swallowed the sentiment with his simmering anger.

"It is a difficult to say, Director," he replied and fought the urge to sneer as he fed Timchenko his own philosophy back to him. "As you said, there are unknown unknowns."

The two seated men made eye contact and conducted a silent exchange—what was understood did not need to be stated. Timchenko rose from the table and the chairman quickly followed suit. "It has been a pleasure, Vladimir, as always," Timchenko said limply, shaking the chairman's hand.

"We will be in touch as things develop," Volsky reassured him while subtly reminding the director that the Ivory Tower was large and contained multitudes.

Konev breathed easier once Timchenko left the room, but remained quiet at Volsky's signal. The chairman waited several seconds after hearing the outer door close before lowering his upheld hand. Once he was certain the SVR director was gone, he softened his demeanor and broke the silence.

"You play a dangerous game, Misha," Volsky cautioned him. "He is not one to annoy."

The captain relaxed a measure with the chairman's familiarity and spoke his mind, "If the SVR had run a better mission, they wouldn't need Ivory Tower to clean up their mess."

Volsky shrugged in resignation. "That is the nature of the game, Misha. We have all put our hands in the fire and gotten burned. This time, it was Director Timchenko's turn. Do not take it personally."

Konev took issue with the older man's conciliatory tone but phrased it gently. "Even you must admit it is a little ham-handed to make a fake ring before making sure the real one doesn't exist. And then, to have the balls to criticize our operations while we are trying to help them recover from their screw up." He shook his head. "I expect better from the SVR."

Volsky laughed at the captain's frank naiveté and exclaimed, "As do we all!" Konev caught a rare glimpse of what the chairman's carefree younger self would have looked like before he knew as much as he did. "We are a people of contrasts, capable of the highest subtleties and the grossest baseness. The uncomfortable truth is that for all our scheming and planning, failure is always an option. Everyone miscalculates at one time or another, but how we recover from those mistakes is what determines how far we go and how long we last."

Volsky lit a cigarette on his way to the massive oak desk and motioned for Konev to take a seat. "Misha, you know that I love you like a son. You are proud, smart, ambitious." He punctuated the list of Konev's attributes with a deep draw. "You want to make your mark and gain glory, and I believe you will, but this mistake of yours..." he trailed off as he rounded the corner and didn't continue until he reestablished eye contact. "Such mistakes end careers. Or lives."

"I can fix this. Personally," Konev asserted emphatically. When his team hadn't reported in, he'd started creating various response scenarios based on all the possible variables he could think of.

Volsky smiled. "Good. Do it. I want to see the mission plans within the hour."

"And what about Director Timchenko?" Konev inquired cautiously.

Volsky gestured with his free hand. "You leave him to me, but remember what I said. Be careful with Timchenko. He is probably the most dangerous person *you* have ever met. He is a killer with the face of a rabbit."

Konev heard Volsky stress the word "you," and his imagination flashed to those above the chairman. It was a whole other echelon of command with which the captain had no experience, and he was grateful that Chairman Volsky was willing to provide him cover. For now, at least.

Konev stood and saluted, and Volsky dismissed him from his office. As the captain rushed through the turquoise and mint halls to his office, the chairman finished his cigarette. After he stubbed out the butt, he picked up his phone and dialed. He had a difficult call to make to Major General Nikolay Yastrzhembsky, General Secretary of the Ivory Tower's Interior Council.

Yastrzhembsky was not technically Volsky's superior, but when blame was doled out in situations like this, the general secretary was the first person to whom Volsky answered. The major general was not pleased to hear the operation to assist the SVR had failed, and just as Konev had to take responsibility for Lieutenant Lokhov—may he rest in peace—Volsky had to take the heat for Konev. The chairman's primary goal was to reassure the general secretary that things were being handled and wrestle control of the narrative from the SVR.

Even as General Secretary Yastrzhembsky received Volsky's report, he wanted independent confirmation of the evolving situation. He was well aware that Director Timchenko wasn't the only one who knew how to play politics and spin information. He needed someone discrete with no affiliation to the mission to give him an honest account.

As soon as the major general was off the line with the chairman, he made another call to the middle darkness of central Russia. Alexander Petrovich Lukin answered on the fifth ring and spoke loudly over the considerable background noise. "Sir," he answered, fully aware of who was calling and that no one else need know such information.

"I need you to follow an agent," Yastrzhembsky ordered.

Lukin looked out over the blue water of the Angara River and focused on the voice on the other side of the line. "Sir, this is a crucial time for the project," he respectfully objected.

"That can wait, at least temporarily. I need you to follow Captain Mikhail Timofeiovich Konev," he dropped the name casually, knowing there was no love lost between the brash young captain and Lukin.

Lukin moved away from the noise before answering. "What is Volsky's whelp up to now?"

"He bungled a mission and I don't want any more mistakes," Yastrzhembsky laid it out plainly. "I know Volsky's covering for him, but I want to know if such confidence is justified. I need you to be my eyes and ears on the ground."

"And where would that be?" Lukin inquired.

The general secretary took that as a yes and smiled. "Luxembourg. I'll arrange transport and send you the pertinent information."

Lukin's mind went to warmer climes—a welcome reprieve from his current assignment. "I'll ready for travel."

Chapter Eight

Gisela Stein looked up from her mobile, puzzled at the sound of tires driving on the gravel of the parking lot. The mail had already been delivered, they weren't expecting any packages, and there were no appointments this late in the afternoon. She signed off with the friend she'd been messaging at her desk and put her phone away in case it was her boss. Working as an office manager at a shipping company wasn't her dream job, but it paid the bills.

RBO GmbH had their start moving coal from the vast mines that littered the North Rhine-Westphalia area and then branched out from there. Centrally located with good access to rail and roads, it was easy enough for RBO to move freight as well as private possessions, as long as the forms were in order. As a modest operation, there were no fancy executive suites or corporate headquarters. Their office was a two-story building on-site next to the open lot that housed the bulk of their cargo.

Despite the title "office manager," she actually didn't have anyone under her to manage. RBO was a small regional company and her job was to keep the paperwork in order, coordinate with the lot on what containers needed to ship when, handle customer service, and keep the office presentable.

Stein opened multiple windows on her computer and made herself look busy while she waited for someone to enter. When the electronic doorbell chimed, it wasn't a workman from the lot or the broad form of Mr. Bergmann that passed through the door. Her visitor was a slim man with short brown hair dressed in a dark gray suit.

She pegging him as a business client or someone who was lost and gave him a neutral smile. "*Willkommen bei RBO. Wie kann ich dir helfen?*"

Haddock visually swept the room, ostensibly to identify the speaker but it was enough to see there were no cameras in the vicinity. "*Es tut mir leid, ich spreche nur ein bisschen Deutsch. Sprechen Sie Englisch?*" he replied in phrasebook German and laid on a thick American accent to sell his mineral engineer cover as an eager but inept speaker.

Her smile warmed. "Of course," she responded in English. "How may I help you?"

"I work for a mining company in the US that is expanding into the European market and I'm investigating shipping options. I understand your company handles freight as well as private shipping for any employees that may need to relocate," he stated directly.

Stein nodded. "That's correct, although the prices vary

considerably based on the nature of the cargo, where it is being shipped to and from, and how it is to be handled en route. If you like, I can make you an appointment to speak to one of our transport specialists."

He bit his lip and shook his head. "I won't be in the area long. I don't suppose there is someone here I could speak to now? Even if it is just a brief meeting to exchange cards and open a line of communication?" he pressed with a dash of his will behind the plea.

"I'm afraid not," she apologized. "Everyone else has gone home for the day and I wouldn't be much help."

He checked the time on his wristwatch while he weighed his options. With any luck, she would have access to the information he needed, and if not, he could make an appointment and try again. "If you have something early tomorrow, I may be able to make it."

"Let me check. Just one moment," she replied courteously as she pulled up the calendar. "I have an opening at 10:15," she offered.

Haddock nodded in agreement. "I think that will work."

She clicked the time slot on the agenda and her screen filled with blank fields. "I just need your details to make the appointment."

Haddock handed her the card he'd prepared earlier. "Everything you need should be on there." She reached out, expecting it to be his business card. It was the right size and weight. However, when she turned her eyes to it, all she saw was a single name handwritten in blue ink: Georgi Kolchak.

It was the name Sebek had given him for the Russian national that purchased the opened letterlock done in the Voynich style. He'd also gotten the name of the company scribbled on the purchase paperwork in the Bulgarian's notes. Haddock had woven a simple charm into the ink on the card as he'd carefully printed the letters, making it easily legible to anyone familiar with the script. Her reading the name closed the magical circuit and his enchantment coursed through her like a jolt of electricity. She froze for a moment, staring at the card.

"Is there anything wrong?" he asked innocently. When she looked up, her brown eyes had a soft haze to them.

"No problem, Mr. Kolchak. How can I help you?" she inquired as if they had just met.

Haddock wove his will into his spoken words and switched to German—one of the many languages in which he was fluent—to make it easier to worm his way into her mind. "My accountant tells me I need receipts and paper records of my shipping activity if I want to include it as a business expense, but I have gone paperless. Do you think you could print something out for me?"

"I understand," she answered back in her mother tongue. "Just let me access your records." She closed the scheduling software and opened client records. "What kind of information do you need?" In her suggestive state, she spoke in an even cadence that was almost singsong.

"Shipping dates, addresses, port fees, container contents," he rattled off a list and Stein nodded docilely. Her subconscious made no objection because everything he'd asked for was consistent with his story and thanks to the initial mesmer, she believed he was Mr. Kolchak.

She clicked a series of tabs before hitting print and handing him a stack of papers. "Will that suffice?"

Haddock quickly flipped through them and smiled when he saw the last shipment was four months ago, which meant the letterlock Sebek had sold Kolchak was somewhere onsite. It was just a matter of finding it before the next container shipped out, which was a herculean task given the size of the pit and the stacks of shipping containers he'd driven past on his way to the office.

"Yes, I think so," he replied and immediately secured them in his briefcase for later examination over a beer and currywurst. "Thank you for your help."

"Of course. Is there anything else?" Stein asked by rote. Even charmed, she performed the patter of customer service.

"No, but could I have my card back?"

She handed back the only physical proof that he'd been there. "Of course. Have a good day, Mr. Kolchak."

"To you as well," he replied as he tucked the card back into his wallet. He added a dollop of magic to his final words.

"Best if you forgot I was here at all." The suggestion permeated through her frontal lobe and sunk into the limbic system. There were so many important things to remember, but this was not one of them.

The electronic ding of the door broke the spell, but Stein's mind was muddled, like waking up from a deep sleep. By the time she oriented herself, the car in the parking lot was already pulling away. *Must have been someone making a U-turn*, her brain filled in the gaps. She checked the time—close enough to five to start winding everything down. She systematically closed all the programs on her computer before putting it to sleep for the day.

Chapter Nine

Wiltz, Luxembourg
8th of September, 1:53 p.m. (GMT+2)

Alexander Lukin knew that the general secretary of the Ivory Tower's Interior Council was concerned when he pulled him from his current project to tail Volsky's protégé, but he didn't fully appreciate the depth until he received his traveling orders. Belaya Air Base was just outside Irkutsk and the general secretary had secured him a seat in a supersonic military jet. He'd never been in a Mikoyan MiG-31 before and a rare streak of childlike wonder washed over his grizzled face as he zipped along the top of the planet. They'd flown so high, he could easily see the curvature of the earth. The 5,200 km flight to Moscow took a mere two hours and ten minutes from liftoff to touchdown, and they had even refueled in the air to save time. Which was another brand-new experience for Lukin.

He didn't grasp the severity of the situation until he read the briefing. It was one thing to make mistakes on an internal operation, but the stakes were higher when collaborating with another agency, especially the SVR. Director Timchenko was not someone to trifle with, and there was no way to hide this slip-up from him.

Such debacles were rarely one person's fault, but Timchenko was doing his best to distance himself and the SVR from the bungled operation, which left the Ivory Tower out on a limb. Considering all the agents on the ground were dead, Captain Konev was in prime position to take the fall.

If Volsky had simply disciplined Konev, it would have stopped the blame from creeping higher up. Everyone could console themselves with the idea that it was the result of one bad widget but once it was removed, the machine was sound. But the second Volsky vouched for Konev, the shadow of incompetence cast more shade—something the general secretary of the Interior Council could not ignore.

It was par for the course in Lukin's experience. A series of poor decisions, negligence, and lack of foresight created a problem and when field agents failed to fix it, responsibility fell hardest on them...but if they had been successful? The lion's share of the credit went to command for employing the right tool.

That wasn't to say Lukin felt sorry for the captain. There was no question that Konev should have known better than to delegate on an operation with the SVR, and the fact that he did supported the notion that Volsky shouldn't have put Konev in charge in the first place. It was sloppy on all counts and there was blame everywhere. Lukin had no doubt that if he'd been in the same position, Volsky would have offered him little shelter from Timchenko's wrath. He'd been in the game long enough to know who his friends were and who would use him as cover in front of a firing squad, which was why he was acting on the general secretary's behalf.

Lukin was a rare breed: a well-seasoned operative. Few made it in the field as long as him. They usually died on the job or got promoted into administrative command as they aged out. In spite of being given the toughest assignments, he wasn't dead yet, and his attempts to move into the upper echelons of command were stymied by those that didn't consider him Russian enough because his parents were German, even though he was born and raised in Russia. WWII had touched every family and while time could heal all wounds, there would always be scars. Those who were not outright ethnically biased took advantage of the sentiment. Lukin was far too effective to commanders who needed results on the ground. Ironically enough, had he been less competent he would not have been in the field anymore.

Lukin parked his rental car in the parking lot of Hotel Le Canard Gris and finished his coffee. He'd traveled seven time zones in nearly as many hours, but now wasn't the time to feel shagged out. He mentally pumped himself up and the jolt of caffeine pushed off the worst of the jetlag. Then, he pulled out his mobile and dialed.

A man answered in French on the second ring, "Le Canard Gris."

"Yes, this is Georgi Kolchak," Lukin replied with a perceptible Russian accent over his grammatically questionable French—Konev's French was only passable. "I have reservation tonight, but maybe need to have package sent. Could you my room number to me tell?"

"Certainly, Mr. Kolchak," the receptionist answered slowly, enunciating each word to make them easier to understand. "If I could have your confirmation number, please?"

"Yes. Just one minute," he replied as he found the long alphanumeric sequence Ivory Tower administration had given him. He parsed the numbers one by one, avoiding the nightmare that was the higher-level French counting system. He could hear the receptionist type in the background.

"Thank you, sir. Your room number is 303."

"Da," Lukin grunted but followed up with *merci* before hanging up and exiting his rental. He removed his luggage from the trunk and strode through the entrance of Le Canard Gris.

As he rolled into the foyer, he gave a short perfunctory nod to the receptionist behind the counter as if he were a paying guest. He summoned the elevator and waited with his back to the man until the carriage arrived. When the pressed the button for the third floor he glanced at the receptionist, who was busy looking down at something, perhaps a book or a phone. Whatever he was doing, he wasn't paying attention to Lukin. *Perfect*, he thought as the doors closed.

The art of disguise was something he'd mastered over the years, both mundane and magical. He'd developed many techniques, but the best ordinary accoutrement by far was the rolling luggage. Its psychological effect was astounding, like holding a subliminal sign that said "Ignore me. I am not a threat nor am I doing anything of interest. I am a merely a humble traveler, weary of this world." Once people clocked the luggage pulled behind him, it made him invisible, even to law enforcement. It was the lowest-cost, highest return disguise his profession could ask for. He never wanted to stand out, never wanted to be looked at twice, and most importantly, never wanted to be remembered. And what was more forgettable than a schmo schlepping luggage?

It didn't just work in the airports, hotels, and train stations. In Europe, people pulled wheelie luggage everywhere thanks to the extensive transit system. It was so ubiquitous that local residents of some cities were trying to ban them due to the racket their wheels made on cobblestones at all hours of the night.

Lukin had timed his entry during the afternoon lull, after check-out and room turnover but before check-in. There would be the fewest number of people inside the hotel and staff would be twiddling their thumbs until check-in time. Once on the third floor, he followed the signs to his destination, making note of the cameras along the way. There were only two on the obvious points of entry—one on the elevators and one on the fire exit—but neither had line of sight to room 303.

He snapped on a pair of transparent latex gloves and opened his luggage for his under-the-door tool. It was little more than a straight yet pliable metal tube with a doubled-back metal wire running through it, but Lukin never went on a mission without it. As long as there was a gap at the bottom of the door and the deadbolt was not engaged, there was no hotel lock and key system that it couldn't mechanically undermine.

He measured the height of the exterior door handle and bent the tube at a 90-degree angle, making it L-shaped with a loop of metal wire on the long side and the drawstrings on the other. He slid the length of metal under the door, and with a practiced hand, he lassoed the interior door handle with the wire as he flipped the tube using the short end of the L. It tightened around the door's handle as he pulled the wire's ends, putting just enough downward pressure to engage the handle inside the room. He then simply pushed the door open with his forehead once the lock's bolt released. He rose from the ground and entered, pulling his luggage behind him. It had taken twenty-three seconds.

He assessed the room for unexpected vulnerabilities that would derail his plan but saw nothing out of the ordinary. He set to work planting two listening devices. The first was a Cold War-style bug placed into the receiver of the room's ancient phone. Although ancient, the bug still worked and the room was small enough for it to pick up any chatter even if it wasn't over the phone, but because it was always on, it was easy to find on a standard sweep. However, its age was part of its disguise. If Konev found it, it could easily be mistaken as a relic from some long-ago operation. It wasn't uncommon in hotels that had been around during the heyday of spying, even in a place as out of the way as this. The scope of Soviet intelligence gathering had been wide and pervasive. They'd never lacked in manpower.

The second listening device was modern and significantly more subtle: a GMS bug integrated into the interior of a pre-aged power strip. It was wireless with a listening radius of 30-50 feet and would be undetectable until Lukin turned it on—accessed by a simple phone call. If Konev did a sweep upon arrival and found the first bug, Lukin would give it a little time and switch on the GMS remotely. He pegged the young captain as brash and over confident, not nearly contentious enough to do another sweep after he'd already found one bug.

Lukin plugged the power strip into an outlet and placed it between the desk lamp and the wall—hidden in plain sight. Then, he pulled out his phone and tuned to their respective channels. Once he'd tested that both were transmitting and he was receiving, he moved to the windows and pulled back the light-blocking curtains. He memorized what would be Konev's range of view and which areas would be safe for surveillance. He set the curtains back to their prior position and exited the room, slipping off his gloves when he was back in the hall and down the elevator. He wheeled past the receptionist with another perfunctory nod and returned to his car.

Chapter Ten

Lukin soaked in the warm sunny afternoon as he drove through the rolling hills of the Ardennes. He'd spent so much time in Siberia as of late that it was nice to see so much vibrant, verdant green. The light dappled through the full canopy as he took the gentle curves that followed a river. Schlass Wollef was only fifteen minutes away by car and he had a few hours before Konev's flight landed—enough time for Lukin to investigate the castle before he arrived.

He took the long way to the near-empty parking lot to get a visual on the castle's exterior, and his tires crunched on the gravel as he parked. There was no avoiding the camera covering the entrance, but his hat and sunglasses obscured most of his features.

The barbican had been converted into a point of entry where guests bought tickets. He opted for the self-guided tour that came with pre-recorded audio. As the woman working the front explained the rules of visiting the castle, Lukin nodded along but was only half-listening. He was all too aware that he was standing in what was historically a killing zone: a fortified corridor with gates and portcullises on either end and murder holes in the ceiling for boiling liquids and unfriendly pointy objects. Schlass Wollef may have become another banal tourist stop, but it had been designed for a much more brutal purpose.

He started on the left as suggested and followed the marked path. The first pass was to get a feel for the place and look for cameras inside, of which there were woefully few. The audio guide worked by scanning codes on strategically placed placards, but it didn't automatically change its narrative when he entered a new area. Just to be on the safe side that it wasn't being tracked, he stashed his unit in the restroom before making a beeline for the library.

Natural light poured in through the vaulted glass ceiling, bathing the central atrium in the late afternoon sun. As there was no one else there, he directly walked to the cast iron spiral staircase that led to the upper levels. It was guarded by a draped velvet rope from which hung a sign: "Do Not Enter" printed in four different languages. He stepped over the rope and climbed two stories in a flash.

Once on the third floor, he put on gloves and hugged the exterior wall until he reached the Carlton House desk. He scanned the area and found the desk warded with fear and apathy—an unexpected complication but nothing beyond what Lieutenant Lokhov should have been able to handle according to his file.

He made quick work of disarming the desk and opening the drawers in their proper sequence. He checked behind the inlay panel and found it empty. Either the ring was never there or the triad had retrieved it. He was inclined to believe the latter as the last reported communication sent from the triad was that the ring had been acquired. So far, he had no reason to doubt the report.

As he bent down to put the panel back into place, he spotted a recess on the underside of the desk. *Isn't that interesting...?* He patted it down and after he found it empty, went over the rest of the desk looking for other hiding spots. When that came up blank, he reset the panels, rearmed the desk, and took off his gloves. Whatever trouble fell upon the triad, it must have come later; the bodies were found in the river, not the library.

He pivoted to return to the public areas and heard something grind under his hard sole on the gap between rugs. He bent down to take a closer look and saw miniscule white grains scattered on the hardwood floor. He collected some in his hand and it was sandy to the touch. There was no odor when he took a sniff, but he recognized the taste when he brought a little to the tip of his tongue. *Salt.*

If it were a kitchen or restaurant, he could overlook a little salt on the floor, but in the library where a now dead Ivory Tower triad had recently conducted a mission? That was too coincidental to be chance. If the signet ring had been enchanted, the presence of salt could be easily explained—some of it had spilt as the triad used it to neutralize its magic during transport. Unfortunately, the ring wasn't magically endowed.

But perhaps whatever was stashed under the desk was? he speculated as he dusted the grit from his hands. Konev hadn't mentioned anything about it in his report and the mission directive had been clear—only take the ring and nothing else—but it was hardly a secret that everyone had a side hustle. People generally turned a blind eye as long as they didn't steal the wrong thing from the wrong people.

Did the triad take something cursed that led to their death? he threw against the wall to see if it stuck. None of them were particularly skilled in the arcane. Kirpichenko had the most potential, but he was early in his magical education and had much to learn. He added it to his mental list of possibilities, but it didn't explain why none of them had any of their possessions when they were dragged out of the river.

The official cause of death was drowning by misadventure, a verdict everyone was willing to accept for a swift and quiet resolution, but Lukin suspected the agents were impaired or unconscious—if not already dead—before they entered the river. How else could their boat have capsized with no trace of their gear or identification on their person? It wasn't like the Sûre had rapids.

As he doubled back to the bathroom to retrieve his audio unit, Lukin hit on another idea: the Salt Mine had been here. The salt on the floor wasn't from neutralizing an object; the grind had been too fine. He wasn't sure what they did with salt, but he always found it when he crossed paths with their agents, even when magical items weren't involved, and recently the grind of the salt had changed from about table salt sized to extremely fine, nearly powdery. The idea opened new lines of inquiry. Were they here by happenstance or to deliberately counter the SVR plot? Did they have the ring and if so, what did they intend to do with it?

If the Salt Mine had intercepted the triad, it was likely on their way out, after they already had the ring. It's what Lukin would have done in their place. No need to risk the desk's magic when you could let others do it. He cursed under his breath and set a course for the battlements. The report said the triad had accessed the castle by river, and there was no better view of the environs than from the castle's tall walls.

There were a few people up top, catching an illicit smoke judging by the occasional spent butt. He planted the headset firmly on his ears, signaling to any passersby that conversation or engagement was not welcomed. He focused his attention to the parts of the wall-walk that would be accessible by river.

The wall-walk's safety railing was bolted into the stone and in need of a new coat of paint, and he casually reached out for it, placing the tips of his finger along the underside. He took a leisurely pace and paused when his hand found a smooth spot along the otherwise flaking surface. Two fingers width of old paint had been sloughed off—just about the width of a grappling hook tine.

He peered over the edge of the rampart just opposite and looked straight down at the ring of sharp and jagged rocks that circled the castle. It was a long way down with one hell of an unfriendly landing. Past the rubble and down the lush forested hillside was the Sûre River, where the bodies of the triad had ended up.

He looked for signs of a struggle on the battlements but the stoic stone gave nothing away. He was tempted to go down and search the area. Any blood would have washed away in the storm cell that passed through in the week since the triad was here, but there could still be signs that the bodies had been moved, and if he was extremely lucky, maybe even the ring itself. Perhaps it had fallen out of a pocket.

But the idea was, logistically, a bad one. The search would go easier with daylight, but then he could also easily be seen from the wall. To do so after the castle had closed would be mean dodging Konev's inevitable search of the area. Lukin reigned in his curious nature and reminded himself of why he was in Luxembourg. He wasn't here to figure out what happened to the triad. His purpose was to be the general secretary's eyes and ears on the ground as Konev tried to fix his error. *Better to watch Konev comb the scene, see what he finds, and compare that with what he reports,* he eventually decided.

He wiped down his audio unit before returning it at the barbican on his way out. His stomach confusingly growled for food: with all the jetlag it wasn't sure which meal was overdue, but it knew it was owed one. He stopped at a supermarket and bought a couple of overpriced sandwiches and a soda to tide him over. As he neared Le Canard Gris, he drove on the back streets and found a suitable observation point that wasn't visible from the main road. He didn't want Konev to drive by and spot him.

Once he was parked, he checked Konev's flight for delays and found it had landed on time. As the sun lowered, he watched the hotel's parking lot with his binoculars in one hand and a sandwich in the other. He'd just finished an over-mayoed affair when a vehicle pulled into the parking lot and backed into a space with the front facing the exit. Lukin recognized good tradecraft when he saw it and zoomed in.

The driver emerged from the newly-parked car. He had the right look: early 30s, six feet tall, dark hair, broad at the shoulders and slim through the waist. It wasn't until he turned his head that Lukin made a positive ID: Konev had arrived. His hair was longer and slicked back, but there was no mistaking that profile. It was so smugly punchable; Lukin had put that kink in his nose himself.

Lukin watched as Konev's deep-set eyes darted to and fro, taking in their surroundings. With no threats perceived, he transformed into no one of interest by sliding on his jacket and dragging his own wheeled luggage behind him.

Lukin tuned into the phone bug and started his car once

he heard Konev enter the room. He parked on the far end of the lot, well out of sight from room 303's view and tutted when Konev failed to even scan the room for listening devices.

Lukin exited his car and, although he had no luggage to hide behind this time, he did have his phone. To the casual observer, he was just another guy listening to someone chew his ear off. As he passed by the front of Konev's car, he bent down under the guise of re-lacing a loose shoe and placed a magnetic GPS tracker underneath the front bumper and then went back to his car to continue to listen as Konev settled in.

*****

Captain Mikhail Konev folded the last of his clothing and placed it in the dresser drawers. Some people preferred to live out of their suitcase when they traveled, but he found it distasteful. He liked to think that wherever he was, that was home for the time being.

In some ways, hotels were better than home. A stack of clean towels, extra pillows, and a tidied room were only one phone call away. He never had to do dishes or laundry. And he enjoyed the freedom of relative anonymity. When he was staying in a hotel, he called the shots, including his identity.

He stashed the empty luggage into the space under his newly hung dressing jackets and started a cup of coffee. As he waited for his brew, he pulled out his phone and searched for nearby restaurants. He would visit the castle before it closed but the ritual was going to be done after dark, and there was no need to work on an empty stomach. When he found something suitable in the general direction of Schlass Wollef, he called and made a reservation for one at 8:00 p.m.

He added sugar and non-dairy creamer until the black sludge became palatable. Hotel coffee wasn't his first choice, but he had work to do. He reviewed the triad's mission plan and what information they had on the bodies. There were no knife or gun wounds and no signs of strangulation, but the blunt force trauma on Lokhov's head could have been from a weapon, even if the Luxembourg medical examiner labeled it as "consistent with expected riverine injury."

He was plotting out his search of the castle's grounds when his phone rang. Konev answered as soon as he saw the name on the screen: Feliks Sebek.

"Hello?" Konev answered in Russian.

"Georgi!" Sebek gregariously greeted him. "It's Feliks, from Ignis Liber."

Konev turned down his phone to compensate for the Bulgarian's excessive default speaking volume. "Feliks, I hope you are calling with good news."

Sebek made a noise with his tongue across the back of his teeth. "Regretfully, no. You have been outbid."

Konev's shoulders slumped. "That's unfortunate. I don't suppose there is a way to increase my bid?"

"Ah, Georgi, you know the rules! I can't do that," Sebek obligatorily objected. "But if I were to make an exception for you, what are we talking about?"

Konev ran the numbers in his head. "Twenty-five percent?"

From his office in Sofia, Sebek smiled. He always called a few losers first to see if they would up their bids. Georgi's increase wouldn't be enough to win, but it did pad Sebek's margin as the best offer leapt upward to overtake Georgi's.

"That may be enough, but I'll have to check," Sebek lied. "Call you right back?"

"That's fine," Konev curtly replied.

"Excellent! *Dochuvane*!" Sebek exclaimed in Bulgarian before hanging up.

Konev checked his bank while he waited for news. Truth be told, raising his bid twenty-five percent was already over budget, but he could move money around to cover it. Three minutes later, Sebek called back and they exchanged bad news: Kolchak's bid still wasn't the highest and the Russian wasn't able to go higher.

"You win some, you lose some," Sebek offered him aphorisms. "But I'll keep you informed if anything else like it comes up, eh?"

"Yes, please do," Konev insisted and hung up before Sebek could blast him with another dochuvane. He checked the time and pulled up a different contact on his phone.

"RBO, how may I direct your call," the receptionist asked

in clipped and precise German.

"Arnold Schmidt, please," Konev responded in kind.

"Who may I say is calling?"

"Georgi Kolchak."

"One minute, Mr. Kolchak," she replied before sending his call to hold. It played a tasteful if stodgy classical music station and he tapped his fingers to the meter while he waited.

"Arnold Schmidt," the man on the line answered.

"Hello, this is Georgi Kolchak. I had called earlier about possibly adding something to the container before shipment?" he jogged Schmidt's memory. "I'm calling to let you know that is no longer happening and I'd like my shipment to proceed on schedule."

"No problem, Mr. Kolchak. If you could give me your customer number, I can arrange all that."

"0875AZ5137-81," Konev rattled off from memory.

"One moment," Schmidt responded as the computer pulled up the file. "I have a single container destined for St. Petersburg."

"That is correct," Konev confirmed. He heard typing and clicking on the other end of the line.

"I have initiated shipping of your container, Mr. Kolchak."

"Excellent. When can I expect delivery?"

"We can get it to Rotterdam tomorrow. Factor in customs and travel time...it should be in St. Petersburg a week from tomorrow," Schmidt guessed and added a caveat, "assuming there are no unforeseen delays." He'd been doing this long enough to know that managing expectations were the key to customer satisfaction.

"Naturally," Konev conceded. "My thanks, Mr. Schmidt."

"Thank you for choosing RBO, Mr. Kolchak," Schmidt said with all the faux enthusiasm a proper German could muster. While Konev made a cryptic addition in his agenda, Lukin was smilingly taking notes of his own inside his car.

Chapter Eleven

Heiderscheidergrund, Luxembourg
8th of September, 10:07 p.m. (GMT+2)

Captain Konev made his way through the lightly wooded terrain on the more remote side of the Sûre River. The moonbeams piercing through the clouds were enough to get him to the tree line, but once he was in the thick of it, the same broad oak leaves that claimed as much sunlight as possible from the dominant pines also blocked out the moon. He loathed to turn on his flashlight and attract attention. Instead, he followed the sound of moving water. As long as he made it to the river, he could proceed with his plan.

He'd made it to Schlass Wollef shortly before it closed for the day, giving him enough time to search inside but ensuring no one would be on the walls when he did his exterior examination in daylight. The library didn't reveal what had happened to the triad, only that they had left the library with the ring and manuscript in hand. Outside, he found some distinctive drag marks leading from castle to the river, suggesting their troubles occurred on the way out. There were no signs of a struggle or chase in the shielded woods, which put the nail in the coffin for him: his team hadn't made it back to the river alive.

Over dinner, he chewed on the implications along with his steak and came to the conclusion that it had to be professional opposition. A run in with opportunistic thieves or petty vandals would have ended differently. Kirpichenko may have been green, but Lokhov and Stashkysnky were both former SVR. They knew how to take care of problems.

More worrisome was the source of the opposition. *Was there an intelligence leak? Was it inside SVR?* Even as he stumbled over tree roots in the dark, Konev toyed with ways he could spin it as such. It would bring him much pleasure to turn the knife back on Director Timchenko.

He breathed a sigh of relief when he could see the silhouette of Schlass Wollef on the other side of the river. The red blinking lights on the top of the lupine towers were blessed beacons guiding him through the canopy cover. Eventually, the woods gave way to the steep, rocky cut bank opposite the castle's point bar.

He clambered down to the water's edge and found a stable perch. From his backpack, he removed an empty plastic water bottle and unscrewed the cap. He crouched down and held it underwater until no more air bubbles rose to the surface. He'd gathered the rest of the ritual components before dinner, but the water had to be fresh. He tightly capped the bottle before scrambling up the bank and retreating behind the tree line.

His plan was to search the river using magical assistance,

namely a river sprite. Sprites were immaterial spirits tied to natural forms in the Magh Meall. Like elementals, their physical forms were comprised of the element they embodied, but they were far from obedient servants. Sprites had a will of their own and were easily placated or entreated when encountered in the middle lands, but they could also turn territorial and aggressive if pressed.

Konev found level ground and withdrew a thick silver bowl from his backpack. Its circumference wasn't much larger than a cereal bowl, but it was deeper. He wiped it down with a cloth and checked the engraving—two infinity signs carved in the center perpendicular to each other: one within and one without. Together, they created a compass rose, albeit separated by a layer of precious metal. Using his compass, he aligned it to the cardinal directions and placed the bowl on the ground before filling it with the water he'd taken from the Sûre.

Next, he placed a hotel towel on the ground and retrieved a newly-purchased pack of Gauloises, a pack of rolling papers, and two bottles of dried herbs. He made a custom blend from the tobacco of a gutted cigarette with a generous line of basil and sage. He licked the edge of the paper and ineptly rolled it into a wobbly snake.

Konev reluctantly lit the end and coaxed the flame into the homemade cigarette with a draw of his breath. The smoke burned his lungs but he stopped himself from coughing. He had his vices, but smoking wasn't one of them. Without a filter, the nicotine hit him hard, but he forced himself to take in as much as he could stomach. He got halfway through before calling it quits and stubbing it out into the damp soil beside him.

After a few breaths of clean air, he focused and intoned in Russian, amplifying his will by speaking in his mother tongue. "Spirits of the water, hear my call!" With slow deliberate movements, he painted and smeared his gathered will into the air. To the uninformed, it looked like he was doing a strange variant of tai chi, and each broad stroke of his palm was accompanied by another supplication.

When he had a metaphysical canvas gessoed with his will, he reached down and dipped his fingers into the bowl. On his forehead, he anointed himself with a wet infinity symbol and made his final entreaty. "Spirits of the water, hear my call!" He waited with bated breath to see if his summoning ritual had worked. He'd done everything right, but that wasn't always enough.

In the center of the Sûre, small ripples bubbled from the deep. Konev couldn't see it in the darkness, but he felt it as it gained momentum. A standing wave rose from the surface in an infinity symbol and the water in his silver bowl roiled sympathetically. When it reached a foot in height, the wave collapsed in a splash, and out of the turbulence emerged a figure. Composed of churning water, the decidedly female form was no more than five feet tall. It had no facial features to speak of, but Konev could tell it was not pleased with being summoned.

"I have heard your call, human. Now hear mine," it icily menaced. As it walked on the river toward Konev, jets of water spurted in arcs from its back, forming intricate patterns that resonated and expressed a musical note, not unlike a singing wine glass but superior to it in all ways. It was lyrical and enticing like a siren's song, beckoning him to be one with the water. He longed to obey; and but for the herbal infusion fortifying his will, his would have been the fourth body the Luxembourg police dredged from the river.

Instead, Konev stood firm on solid ground and puffed out his chest in defiance. "I have but a small task. The sooner you perform it, the sooner you can return to your home."

It formed a spear of will and probed for weak spots to exploit with its charms but was met with the shield of his plastered will. After a brief contest of attack and defense, it asked, "What do you command?" Without its frosty tone, the voice sounded like water rolling over a spillway—forceful but not threatening.

"I seek three items from the water. The first is a manuscript, the separated pages of an old book now cut loose from its bindings. The second is a phone like this one," he held up his to show the sprite, "but the one I seek will be encased in green. The last object I seek is a silver ring bearing a lion inscribed in a red stone." Konev pointed toward the castle. "I command you to search from the bend west of the castle on that hill all the way to the dam in the east for these things."

"As you wish," the sprite burbled before sliding back into the water.

Konev sat back on the hotel towel while he waited. He passed the time mentally composing his mission report to Chairman Volsky, one that pointed the finger back to SVR. Then, he remembered his mentor's advice and decided on a subtler touch, merely mentioning that SVR was one possible source of a leak. He patted himself on the back for that and had figured out most of what he wanted to say and how to say it by the time the sprite resurfaced.

It stayed on the Sûre and formed a long tentacle of water to jettison a lone mobile phone at Konev's feet. "I have done as you've asked," it obliquely reminded him of their deal.

"And you're sure the other two items weren't in the river?" Konev grilled her.

"If they were, I would have brought them," it replied sharply. *Humans!*

Konev walked the silver bowl to the edge and poured the water out. "Then consider your service complete." As the last drop fell and rejoined the river, the spite smiled and returned to its home in the middle lands.

Once he was certain the sprite was gone, he released his will and put away the ritual gear. He picked up the wet mobile and considered his next move. The triad used a color coded system on missions: green for team leader, yellow for middle operative, and red for the least-experienced. It made for rapid identification of whose phone was whose.

The phone was bricked and the SIM card was still inside, meaning whoever attacked the triad didn't need it. Reporting this could help strengthen a claim that it was an SVR leak, but then he would have to turn over Lokhov's phone as proof. The problem was that it hadn't been in the water long enough to prohibit the skilled Ivory Tower technicians from recovering its data, including his private messages to Lokhov about the manuscript.

After running down his options, Konev hurled the phone back into the river, He grumbled about his luck as he trudged back to his car. He knew finding the ring or the manuscript in the river was a long-shot after what he'd found earlier today, but he was still disappointed. It would have made everything easier.

A hundred meters away, Lukin lowered his black, fur-shielded, mini-parabolic microphone as Konev entered his vehicle. The microphone wasn't needed anymore: Lukin's phone would pick up anything interesting on the GMS bug he'd planted under the driver's seat while Konev was eating dinner.

The captain had done what Lukin expected, but the order in which he listed the items to the sprite spoke volumes about Konev's hierarchy of importance. Even when tasked with cleaning up a failed mission, he was more focused on salvaging a manuscript than the mission objective—a manuscript that wasn't mentioned in any report.

And then he tossed the phone back in the water.... Lukin lingered on that as he sat in the darkness under the trees.

If he wanted to know what was more important to Konev than a mission objective, he needed to find a silversmith who could engrave a sprite-summoning bowl on short notice so he could get his hands on that phone. Lukin also needed to find out who Feliks from Ignis Liber was. There was no doubt in Lukin's mind he could be bought. Every man had a price. It was just a matter of tracking him down and hammering out an amount.

Lukin checked his phone for the location of Konev's car. It was on the main road headed back to Wiltz, blissfully unaware it was being tracked. *Makes my job easier!* He laughed at Konev's expense as he packed up and started toward his own car.

Chapter Twelve

Titz, Germany
9th of September, 11:35 a.m. (GMT+2)

Teresa Martinez—codename Lancer—drummed her fingers on the dashboard for want of anything better to do.

"YYZed," Haddock replied in proper Canadian English before she got to the third bar. "Rush? You're going to have to do better than that," he teased her as he looked through the binoculars.

She scoffed. "This coming from the man who played Phil Collins earlier." She picked up her empty coffee cup, hoping it had somehow magically refilled itself since the last time she'd checked. It hadn't.

After catching a red-eye flight to Frankfurt and a high speed train to Cologne, she found doing surveillance in a parked car rather anti-climactic. From the briefing, she'd expected more cloak and dagger: dead nobility, a lost signet ring found, Ivory Tower operatives, a newly discovered section of a cryptic enchanted manuscript, and assumed identities on both sides. It had all the elements of a Gilbert and Sullivan opera, which was apropos for Haddock. He was a consummate actor, even when there was no audience. There was even an air of the theatrical in his plan, for which she was brought in as support.

Haddock had found more security than he'd anticipated after casing out RBO's yard—nothing insurmountable, but it certainly required more specialized equipment than he had on hand. Unfortunately, he didn't have the luxury of time. The container was shipping out of Rotterdam at the end of the week and operationally speaking, grabbing the letterlock from within the Dutch port would be an even bigger nightmare.

The port of Rotterdam was Europe's largest sea port and occupied forty square miles. The complex was subdivided into five concessions operated by different companies with three distribution parks. Once the container entered the port, just finding it would be difficult. And even if they *could* pinpoint where the container was, there was always a lot of traffic inside because the port was open 24/7. Security was also more robust because once something entered Rotterdam, it was free to travel through all of the EU member states: it was an officially sanctioned external border of the European Union and port security checked for a wide array of infringements from safety, smuggling illegal cargo, and tax assessment.

As if all of that wasn't enough, the Salt Mine had informed him that Georgi Kolchak was none other than Captain Mikhail Konev, a known Ivory Tower operative. Haddock's best guess was that this was the captain's private enterprise because if it were Ivory Tower business, it would have been handled by one of their established couriers instead of a small regional German company. Since Haddock didn't have a large enough realized threat to implement institutional attention with a high-profile operation, he had no alternative. He had to hit the container in transit.

"You're sure it's moving today?" Martinez inquired. Freight wasn't like commercial package delivery. There was no app to track one's shipping container.

"They have to move it today if they want to have any hope of loading it on the boat on time," he reasoned.

"Which is the long way of saying no," she goaded him.

"Brat," he shot back without taking his eyes off the yard. The stacks were five high with a heavy duty crane to extricate buried containers. There were single shipping containers on the ground but none of them had been loaded on trucks yet.

"I'm just saying, there better be a whole lot of beer at the end of this. And pretzels with mustard. Maybe a schnitzel?" she added whimsically as she rummaged through her bag for snacks.

"Now you're just listing German things. Next you'll say bratwurst and Black Forest cake," he chided. "We'll be in the Netherlands when this is over, so you'll have to settle for *biertjes* with *bitterballen*."

Martinez made a dubious face. "Not sure I trust a food with the word 'bitter' in it," she commented before chomping a piece of beef jerky.

"You know corn fritters or fried mac and cheese balls? It's like that except with beef and gravy inside," he informed her. "Second only to sandwiches, fried foods dipped in sauce is a favorite among the Dutch." The blinking reverse lights of a truck caught his attention. He sat a little straighter as it squared off with one of the containers and tilted its platform down. "We've got activity."

The driver exited the vehicle, threaded chains through the container's corners, and hooked them to a heavy bar that was attached to the truck. With a press of a button, the wench slowly dragged the shipping container up the inclined plane. Once the bulk of the container was solidly on the platform, the driver engaged the hydraulics, decreasing its angle until the back was level. Physics took over and lifted the far end of the metal box off the ground. The wench pulled it the rest of the way until it was completely on the truck. It was a flawlessly choreographed maneuver that took less than two minutes from start to finish.

The driver secured the container to the platform with chains before reentering the cab. As the loaded vehicle drove toward the front gate, Haddock zoomed in on the numbers painted on its side—it was Kolchak's box, packaged and bound for St. Petersburg. "That's our container."

Martinez turned the engine over and pulled onto the road. It was two hundred plus kilometers to Rotterdam, a straight shot on the highway but she wanted to tail the truck in case it decided to make any detours or take an alternate route. The area was pretty undeveloped with clusters of houses and farms dotting the landscape. From her perspective, there wasn't much difference between the Dutch and German side of the border, but she kept that to herself. She was pretty sure both groups would take offense—something Haddock would feel compelled to point out.

Once they were within the Netherlands, Haddock pulled out the slip of paper that was supposed to help him find the letterlock once he was inside the unit. A standard twenty-foot-long ISO container held a lot of cargo and he'd requested something to speed up the search. His Spidey sense was useless because the Voynich magic had given him the metaphysical cold shoulder, and the hag stone he'd been given to recover literature from Schlass Wollef wouldn't help because it relied on the object being in clear view. Even if the letterlock wasn't packed in cellophane on a pallet, Sebek would have wrapped it in one of his signature conservator's cloth before putting it into another container.

The obvious choice would have been Weber's magical tracker, but that was categorically rejected by both Chloe and Dot because it required cutting out a small piece of the Voynich manuscript to attune the compass. Purposefully damaging a work that didn't need destroying was an anathema to the librarians, and they were additionally cautious since they didn't really understand what the manuscript's magic was about and thought it best not to go cutting before they really knew what was being cut.

With a little lateral thinking, Dot figured out a way to use the Voynich magic without harming the original documents. Haddock wouldn't need to sense the letterlock if she could get it to reach out to him. The magic was woven into the language, and while Dot couldn't reproduce the Voynich enchantment, she could write the script. As she penned a few letters, she cast a little sympathetic magic of her own and kept the message short and sweet: *Find me.* She banked that if the letterlock was genuine, it would be thrilled to find someone that spoke its language, like an immigrant hearing their native tongue after years in exile.

Haddock took off his gloves and placed the paper on his bare hand. As he traced over the letters with his siphoned will, the ink disappeared from the paper and appeared on his palm.

"Any reason you didn't do that earlier?" Martinez asked as she closed in on the truck.

He put away the blank slip and slipped on his glove. "Because someone else's magic itches like crazy."

"Is it going to work?" she wondered. Dot had given a lot of qualifiers when she handed it over.

Haddock gave her a grin. "We'll find out soon enough." He unzipped his jacket revealing the Dutch police uniform underneath. The yellow horizontal strips circled just under his clavicle and across his shoulder blades. *POLITIE* was emblazoned on his chest and back with the flame and law book over the subset O. That was Martinez's cue to turn on the siren and lights, and that drew the driver's attention. He nervously looked in his mirrors as he put on his hazards and pulled over at the first available shoulder.

It was a calculated move to stop the truck in the Netherlands. The company and its staff were German and Haddock figured the driver would be less familiar with Dutch rules and law enforcement even though they were neighboring countries. He rolled the window down as Haddock approached.

"Turn off your engine and exit the vehicle," Haddock said in Dutch.

"My Dutch is not good. Do you speak German?" the driver asked.

"Of course," Haddock replied and repeated his instructions in Dutch-accented German. The heavy-set German complied and glanced at the woman standing behind the officer. She was tall and held herself proud against the wind of traffic that blew the ends of her buttoned jacket and wavy brown hair akimbo. She had an air of authority but wasn't wearing anything that marked her as Dutch police.

Haddock introduced his accomplice. "This woman is from Interpol. She needs to ask you some questions, but she only speaks English."

"British?" he guessed because there was a ferry between the Netherlands and the United Kingdom.

"American," Haddock corrected him.

The German's brow furrowed. *Interpol from America?* He didn't know exactly was what Interpol did, but he knew that they dealt with next-level trouble. Interpol took down transnational criminal operations, which meant this wasn't a routine traffic stop.

The driver directed his attention to Martinez and addressed her in English. "I speak English. What do you want to know?"

Martinez flashed her ID, her way of using her credentials without using Interpol resources that could alert Ivory Tower. "We have had an anonymous tip about trafficking illegal cargo." She intentionally left it vague, leaving the details to the driver's imagination: *Drugs? People? Guns? Consumer goods that eluded VAT?* "I need to see your license, registration, and any paperwork you have on the container."

"My documents are in the cab," the driver explained before moving for the door. He didn't want to give them the impression he was doing a runner. He gave Martinez his papers before pulling out his phone.

Hail Mary, full of grace… "Who are you calling?" Martinez asked sharply. He froze under her hard stare.

"I have to phone this into my company," he said meekly.

"We prefer you didn't do that, sir," she insisted. Her tone informed him this was not a request, but an order. The royal we added linguistic gravitas that was heightened by the steady stream of magic she was pumping his way. "If we find contraband onboard, someone from your company could be involved and your call would only tip them off."

"Yes, I see. I hadn't thought of that," he mumbled as he put the phone back in his pocket. Martinez eased off the reel once she knew she had him on the hook. "Just let the officer do a quick sweep and if there is nothing wrong, you will be free to go on your way."

The driver nodded. It seemed reasonable to him: there was no need to create further delays unless there was something wrong. "It's locked. You'll need these to open it," he told Haddock as he handed him the massive bolt cutters. The industry had moved away from private locks and instead used bolt seals with unique serial numbers to track when a container's contents were accessed in transit. Haddock strode to the back once Martinez had given him the sign that she had the driver well in hand.

He carefully studied the bolt seal before snapping through the metal and pulling it from the lock rod; the more senses he engaged, the easier it would be to magically mend it after he was finished. He released the vertical bars from their sheath and opened the right hand door. The beam of his flashlight illuminated the darkness and he climbed in.

There were pieces of furniture and large boxes along one side, but the bulk of the eight-foot wide container was dedicated to a restored '57 Mercedes SL Pagoda. The sleek silver curves of its long front gleamed in the light. Under different circumstances, he would have spent more time with it—it was truly a thing of beauty—but he wasn't here to steal a car.

He channeled his will into his palm, powering Dot's enchanted ink. He held out his hand and walked down the length of container, waiting for the letterlock to make itself known. With his will extended, he felt something that was equal parts sonar ping and dousing rod. He followed the signal until his hand rested on the back of the Mercedes.

The black soft top was up, and he shined his light through the windows. The red leather interior was empty and the door unlocked. Unfortunately, there was no mechanism for popping the trunk. He propped up his flashlight and pulled out his lock picks, ignoring the growing itch on his palm.

He worked carefully not to scratch the lock. It was more than simply not wanting to leave evidence of tampering. It was against his ethnos to mar such an exquisite piece of art. After a little finesse, the trunk opened to an assortment of smaller boxes within. He slowly passed his hand over the lot until his hand vibrated along with his will, like a metal detector that had hit pay dirt. He picked up the slim box just underneath his palm and verified the sender as Ignis Liber.

Haddock slipped the package under his vest, closed the trunk, and locked it. Then, he placed his lockpicks in his pocket and doubled back. He closed the door and secured the vertical poles before holding the lock rod in place. The itching grew more persistent with the package so close to his person that he had to rub his gloved palm against his thigh before focusing on the cut bolt. With a whisper of his will, he coaxed the sheered metal to knit itself together from the outside in and then convinced the plastic sheathing to reseal the bolt against the elements. Once he was certain it would hold, he rounded the back corner of the truck and gave Martinez a firm nod—item recovered and their farce was coming to an end.

"It's clean," Haddock informed them as he handed the bolt cutters back to the driver.

"Does that mean I can go?" he eagerly asked the officer in German.

"That's not for me to decide," he replied with a quick flit of the eye in Martinez's direction. The German put away the tool as he waited for her judgment.

She sighed and reluctantly returned all his documentation. "Thank you for your cooperation. You're free to go."

Relief washed over the driver. "No problem. I just need to put on a new bolt seal and have you sign as the person that opened the container with a reason for why it was opened."

Martinez cast out more of her will. "That won't be necessary. The container was never opened and all your paperwork is in order."

The driver's mind writhed under her charm. He believed her but something wasn't right. He pointed his thumb to the officer. "Then why did he need bolt cutters?"

Haddock gave him an odd look and spoke to him in

German. "I don't have any bolt cutters. Are you feeling all right?"

The driver took a look in the cab and saw his bolt cutters where he always kept them. *Why did I think the police had them?* he wondered. "Of course, my mistake," he feigned certainty despite his confusion. All he wanted to do was get back on the road and deliver his payload. "I'll be on my way," he reassured the officer as he climbed back into his truck.

Am I going crazy? he wondered as he ran over the events again. He dug out the bolt serial number and waited until the pair got back in their vehicle and drove off before exiting the cab. He had to see for himself. When he found the seal in place and verified the number matched, he silenced the doubt in his mind. *Everything is in order.*

When he got back in his truck, he thought about phoning in the stop. It was protocol to report any deviation during delivery, but nothing was opened and no citations were issued. It was only then that he realized he didn't know the name of the Dutch police officer or the American from Interpol. He put his phone away, shifted his truck into gear, and resumed his route to Rotterdam. *Why look for trouble where there is none?*

Chapter Thirteen

Detroit, Michigan, USA
10th of September, 4:50 p.m. (GMT-4)

Leader sat at her desk, whittling away at the stack of paperwork that had collected since the last time she'd surfaced and spent a work day as Angelica Zervo, CEO of Discretion Minerals. The penthouse office was covered in expensive furniture and modern decor, a consumptive display befitting an executive of her standing. It was part and parcel of the alias she'd cultivated over the decades, along with the power suits, luxury cars, and fine dining. As she signed the last of the flagged signature lines, she buzzed her assistant.

"Yes, Ms. Zervo?" Ethan Helms's thin voice answered the electronic summons.

"I'm finished. You can review it now and see if there is anything missing before I leave for the day." It was her way of informing him she wouldn't be in this office tomorrow.

"As you wish, Ms. Zervo," he replied automatically. In less than a minute, the slim blond had entered, collected the documents, and left.

Leader rose and stretched her legs. She looked out the

window and smiled at the late afternoon sun. As far as she was concerned, that was the nicest part of the suite. She tugged at her collar and undid the top button and sleeves. She'd been in business meetings all day and had to dress for the part, and she was looking forward to changing out of her corporate costume and into a pair of worn jeans, a soft linen tunic, and warm cardigan.

She was accustomed to taking off and putting on identities. Over the years, she'd gone by many names. Even Leader was an invention of convenience. As much as she hated the kabuki, compartmentalization made it easier for everyone.

A light blinked on her phone console and she answered with a curt "Yes."

"Everything looks in order, Ms. Zervo," Helms politely informed her.

"Good. Do you have everything you need to type up the minutes and prepare the contracts?" she asked, giving her assistant one last chance to access her personage.

"Yes, Ms. Zervo," he confirmed.

She let out a small smile and her gray eyes danced a little. "Then I'll be on my way." She slid her short arms into her jacket sleeves and grabbed her briefcase before exiting her office. On the other side of the door, Helms stood waiting for her.

"I've summoned the elevator for you. Have a good evening, Ms. Zervo." When she scanned the area, there was no hint of the mountain of paperwork he'd just taken from her office.

Everything had already been put away; Helms was nothing if not efficient.

"Thank you, Ethan." She nodded in acknowledgement. "I'll be back in the office early next week. You know where to reach me if something comes up."

She entered the elevator and rode down to the parking level. There she changed carriages and presented her titanium key. The elevator lowered into the earth.

Angela Abrams put away her magazine and straightened her posture when she saw Leader was coming down in the screen next to her. There were few exceptions to security protocol, and Leader was one of them. Her person but not her possessions were subject to scanning, and it piqued Abrams's curiosity—what did she have in that briefcase of hers?

"Hello, Angela," Leader greeted her to which Abrams merely smiled and nodded. Abrams was generally a chatty sort, but she had long learned that silence was the best policy when dealing with the boss. Once the scan finished, Leader crossed the threshold and entered the Salt Mine.

First, she went to the fourth floor and checked in with David LaSalle, who was busy working at his desk, his broad shoulders hunched over the computer while his long facile fingers dashed across the keyboard. As soon as the elevator doors opened, all typing stopped and he immediate rose to greet her. "Leader."

"Hello, David," she addressed her assistant-slash-bodyguard and motioned for him to follow her into her office. It was a stark contrast to the one she'd just left, but all things considered she preferred this one. There was a something refreshing about crisp saline walls and uncluttered, spartan decor. LaSalle secured his station and followed her into her office, closing the door behind him.

"Did the package arrive?" she asked.

"At 3:31 p.m.," he responded without needing to ask which package. Leader was keeping close tabs on the Voynich situation.

She checked the time on her watch and did the math. "Ninety minutes? The twins should have the long and short of it by now," she said drily. LaSalle didn't reply but broke his normally serious facade with a brief smirk. Leader didn't share many moments of levity and it felt wrong not to honor it, even as it passed.

"Any developments in the field?" she asked as she put her things away.

"The analysts picked up Ivory Tower movement. Captain Konev—aka Georgi Kolchak—returned to Russia this morning," he reported.

Her gray eyes narrowed and a lone eyebrow raised. "And Major Lukin?"

He felt into their terse, just-the-facts patter. "Midair to Moscow."

"Stigma and Lancer?"

"The Hague. The Letterlock Museum was a bust and they

are awaiting further instructions."

She nodded. With the Ivory Tower back on their own turf, she didn't feel the need to pull Stigma and Lancer out just yet. "I'll be visiting the sixth floor for an update. There may be new directives for them after that." LaSalle heard the finality in her tone and took his leave.

She changed out of her suit and into her casual wear as soon as she was alone. After shedding the last vestiges of Angelica Zervo, she reviewed her real work. LaSalle kept the Salt Mine running smoothly, but she had a lot of irons in the fire. Not all of them could be—or should be—delegated. Once she was satisfied there was nothing pressing, she grabbed her things and headed for the sixth floor.

"Will you need me to escort you anywhere tonight?" LaSalle inquired as she walked to the elevator.

"I don't think so, but I'll call if that changes," she replied before holding her palm and retina to the scanners and pressing the button for level six.

When she'd started the Salt Mine, there was no level six. None of this existed except in her imagination. She made it a reality. Many that started the journey with her were gone, but there were precious few that remained. Chloe and Dot were two of them.

True to form, the twins were having what they regarded as an academic debate, but everyone else would call an argument. Leader had known them long enough to know this was just a small bicker. She'd been witness to more than one real dust up.

Chloe was the first to see her approach and addressed her with a hypothetical, "Can two people with the same prior assumptions hold opposing posterior beliefs?"

"Or does having opposing posterior beliefs mean that they do not—in fact—have the same prior assumptions," Dot countered.

Leader put up her hands. "I have no opinion on the matter. I'm just here to find out where you guys are on the Voynich manuscript. I've got two agents hanging out in the lowlands and I either need to bring them in or give them some direction."

Chloe and Dot exchanged looks and tacitly agreed to a ceasefire. "Everything's laid out over there." Chloe motioned to one of the reading tables.

"I've finished reading the manuscript—including the newly discovered twenty-first quire. The translation should be on your desk," Dot followed up. In unison, the sisters descended from their chair behind the circular desk.

"I saw it on my way in but didn't have a chance to read it yet. I spent all day topside," Leader explained with a hint of lament. "Can you give me the broad strokes?"

"It's part guidebook and part instruction manual," Dot fielded the request. "There's a whole lot of information about flora, fauna, celestial bodies, and astrological movements but it never actually names a location and none of it correlates to anything in the mortal realm."

"Current or historical," Chloe added.

Leader yielded to the librarians' vast knowledge and didn't insult them by asking if they were sure. "What about the instructive part?"

"That's a little more clear cut," Dot replied. "They are alchemical recipes, but most of them use ingredients I've never heard of."

"The plants and animals referenced earlier in the work," Chloe clarified.

"Most of them?" Leader glommed onto Dot's qualifier. Both sisters were precise with their word choices.

"I recognized some of the components found in the twenty-first quire. Once I had written out the translation, Chloe was able to help me track down the ones I didn't know," the surly blonde begrudgingly gave her sister credit.

Leader put on gloves and flipped through quire twenty-one. "What else is in here besides recipes?"

Dot searched for the right description. "Little notes and asides, almost like an extended postscript or footnotes at the end of a scholastic work."

"Only a lot less organized," Chloe asserted. "The last entry was a recipe for ink."

Leader turned to the final page even though she couldn't read it. "Interesting," she commented without knowing precisely why the odd detail seemed significant. She moved her gaze to the single page that had arrived this afternoon through overnight express post from the Netherlands. "And the opened letterlock that isn't a letterlock?"

Dot swelled with pride. "It's the missing sixteenth quire, and someone went to a lot of trouble to hide it."

The forgery at Yale had twenty-eight folios that were unaccounted for, but the Salt Mine had tracked down all but two over the years. Quires sixteen and eighteen were single-paged inserts that had been lost sometime after reorganization and folio numbering, a fact that wasn't suspicious at first glance because the number of pages in any given quire was variable throughout the manuscript. However, once Dot could actually read the work, she'd suspected the quires had been removed on purpose, and quire sixteen was proof positive of her theory.

She pointed out two areas on the page. "Someone magically removed the quire and folio number." Leader ran her laser will over the vellum and the arcane erasure marks lit up in her enhanced sight, as if someone had traced each pen stroke with white-out instead of blocking out the whole section.

"Someone deliberately removed quire sixteen, eighteen, and twenty-one?"

"Yes, but maybe not the same someone. Quire twenty-one still has its quire number but was removed before folio numbering," Chloe pointed out.

"What's so special about quire sixteen?" Leader wondered.

"May I?" Dot asked before taking the single page in gloved hands. She rapidly started making folds, using the steps she'd figured out on the printout. Something niggled at Leader as she watched Dot manipulate it. There was something familiar about the oblique angles and turns but she couldn't quite pin it down.

Dot placed the end product in front of Leader and used her pinky finger as a pointer. "See these two slits? I think you're supposed to weave something through them and these holes highlight specific letters."

"Like a decoder," Chloe elaborated.

"And that something is quire eighteen," Leader surmised. "But that would make it quite narrow."

"Two and a half inches wide—" Dot gave precise dimensions.

"Or a page that is folded down to two and a half inches," Chloe chimed in.

Dot acknowledged her sister's point with a nod before continuing. "Either way, it would explain why we never found either of them before. Quire sixteen wasn't the same dimensions as the rest of the manuscript and I think it's a safe guess that neither is quire eighteen."

Leader traced her finger along the rim. "And what's this say?"

"Follow the path and do not stray." Dot translated.

Leader stepped back and started pacing. The movement helped her think. *Guidebook…instructions…recipes…follow the path…* It circled in her brain and each pass brought her a little closer to the brink of something. She paused mid-stride and returned to the table. "Can you unfold that and refold it again, only this time slower?"

Dot and Chloe exchanged looks. Leader was onto something; best not to break her flow with questions. "Sure."

Leader watched intently as Dot disassembled the figure and reassembled it. Her eyes lit up. "One more time," she requested.

Dot gave her a sour look. Patience was not one of her virtues.

"Indulge me," Leader requested sweetly.

"I'm sure she'll tell us once she's sure," Chloe gently bridged them to common ground.

"Of course," Leader promised, "but we all know no good comes from speaking prematurely." Chloe held back a smile at the carefully measured banality of the response.

Dot's hands repeated themselves a third time and when she was finished, Leader clapped her hands and barked a short laugh. "It's a key!"

Chloe and Dot gave her puzzled stares, but being the diplomatic one, it was Chloe who spoke. "We know. We told you about the decoder."

"Not the quire," Leader said dismissively. "The whole thing. It's a key, with a capital K: a magic that is tied to language that cannot be read unless the reader is attuned to it. A language that—once understood—unlocks that magic."

Dot was the first to catch on. "It would be like writing

everything down in our twin language."

Chloe tilted her head to one side, unconvinced. It stank of sixteenth century occultist hokum, and she held no truck with that.

"Can you think of a better way for a magician to secure their work?" Dot argued and Chloe reluctantly shook her head.

"Why did you have me fold this so many times?" Dot questioned Leader.

"There's a repeating pattern to it, a fae fractal if you will. It took me a while to recognize it in this application, but they use it all the time: music, literature, dance, art, architecture, you name it," she explained. "Think of it as the fae equivalent of the golden ratio."

"Are you saying a fae wrote this?" Chloe asked incredulously. "How would that even be possible? They'd have to have written it in the mortal realm because the karmic cost of bringing something like this from the Magh Meall or Land of Fae would be astronomical."

Dot shook her head. "I don't think a fae wrote this. Fae sigils are purely telepathic. Why go through the trouble of making syntax, grammar, and spelling? That's a lot of unnecessary work."

Leader sighed. As always, the twins made good points. She approached from a different angle. "What if someone created the language and integrated fae-style telepathy?"

The sisters mulled it over. "Maybe that's possible, but who

would know how to do that without actually being fae in the first place?" Chloe tested the theory's weak spots.

"Maybe a human-faerie hybrid that was raised in the Magh Meall but lived in the mortal realm," Dot grasped at straws. She might as well have suggested a unicorn as they were just as rare.

A Cheshire grin came over Leader's face; she knew she'd figured something out but she didn't quite know what it was yet. "What if someone found a fae that was willing to talk?"

"Without incurring the wrath of the noble houses?" Chloe objected. The methods used in telepathic written communication were a closely guarded secret among them.

A *click* went off in Leader's head and now she knew. "Maybe they were already in trouble," Leader lay out a trail of breadcrumbs. "Morc mac Dela was imprisoned for eons for making deals with fiends. And what half-fiend, half-human wizard do we know of who spent a lot of time roaming the Magh Meall?"

"Merlin?!" Chloe and Dot exclaimed at the same time.

Leader's salt and pepper hair bobbed as she doubled down on her idea. "It sounds like something he'd do, doesn't it? Write all this stuff down about some other realm and key it to his own magical language to protect it."

Dot ran with it. "And then someone—maybe even Merlin himself—took out the parts that explained how to actually travel there."

Chloe spoke in a soft pensive voice. "But that would mean this whole time, the thing we've been calling the Voynich manuscript is the Morcandian Key."

All three women sat stunned for a moment as it sunk in. The Morcandian Key was a thing of legend, something referenced as hearsay but no one had actual firsthand experience of it. To learn that it could be real was shocking in-and-of itself, but to think that it could have been sitting in their stacks for decades was almost too much to fathom.

Leader spoke first. "We've got to move all of this somewhere safe."

Dot followed. "We could make a new chamber downstairs and start on the wards tonight"

"But not too close to Excalibur," Chloe qualified.

Dot glared at her. "Obviously."

"And quire sixteen and twenty-one should be stored apart from the main manuscript, just in case there was a good reason they were separated," Leader thought out loud. The librarians nodded in agreement. "Do you two think you can handle it yourselves?"

The set up was too much for Dot to resist. "Why, you got a date?" she sarcastically quipped.

Leader scoffed at the idea. "No, but I know where I can go for answers, if there are any to be had. We still have to find the last quire." There was no question in any of their minds that it had to be found and that they should be the ones to do so.

"Go. We've got this," Chloe spoke for the two of them.

While Chloe and Dot discussed the most suitable place to excavate a new containment cubbie in the Mine's lower levels, Leader picked up the phone and dialed the fourth floor. A crisp tenor answered on the second ring. "David, change in plans. I'll need your service this evening after all."

Chapter Fourteen

The Magh Meall
Summer Epoch

Under the setting purple-tinged light of the middle lands stood a mound, ten feet tall and a hundred feet in diameter. At its center rose an ash tree whose vast canopy spread high and wide. Within the earth, Morc mac Dela sat alone in the dark. He was once again made captive by his distant progeny.

He was intimately familiar with every inch of the three lightless stone-lined rooms that were his prison, but this time, they had left him nothing. All his possessions were cleared out when he'd escaped and his spear was stripped from him by a bolt of lightning upon recapture.

His sensitive ears perked up at a sound emerging out of the silence: footsteps. He immediately rose and approached the two stone slabs that sealed him inside the tumulus. He tested their strength with his formidable will and found them solid, humming with the ancient arcane power of the ley lines that lay beneath the mound.

From the other side, he heard a voice call him by name, "Morc mac Dela." He didn't recognize it and couldn't get a read on the speaker through the magically reinforced doors. After his latest escape, back-up measures were put in place should the ley lines bend again.

"Aye," he answered. "Who comes to my door?"

"One who would like a word with you," Leader responded without identifying herself.

He honeyed his words with his will and called out, "Then all you have to do is enter." The short laugh that followed wasn't nearly lyrical or cruel enough to be one of his seed, which narrowed the field of possibilities considerably.

"That wasn't very nice," she chided him. "Perhaps you are not amenable to company. Would you rather I left?"

"No," he immediately spoke. Distraction was hard to come by and whoever she was, she was bold. She knew his name, so she must know his power, yet she dared to approach him. It was clear she wanted something from him; all his visitors did. Perhaps she knew something that would interest him. "What is it that you want to talk about?"

"Many have come to you for knowledge over the ages, and not all of them were faeries. I want to know anyone with whom you have shared the secret of writing by intent," Leader spelled out her request directly.

He played coy. "And what would you give me in exchange?"

Leader proceeded with caution. "What do you want to know?"

"Something big ripped through the middle lands recently.

Even in this tomb, I felt its reverberations. I want to know what caused it," he bargained.

She weighed his price. There was no question that she could now speak of the events that precipitated the fall of House Dela, the noble lineage directly descended from the imprisoned Fomoir who gave them their name. Titania's curse of silence had lifted once Alberia returned, but knowledge was power. Even caged, Morc mac Dela was dangerous. However, there were many ways of recounting what happened earnestly without giving away much, which swayed her to agree.

"Only if you answer first," she stated her condition.

The Fomoir consented by addressing her initial query. "Long ago, someone came to me to learn the ways of fae writing, but I do not know his name." The fae were well known for their ability to say the truth without revealing all—something they'd inherited from their progenitors, the Fomoire.

"How did he call himself?" she followed up.

"Ah," he stopped her. "First, tell me what happened to cause the earth to shake."

He wants tit for tat, Leader parsed his intent and judiciously replied, "Justice was dispensed." Morc mac Dela smiled. Clearly, he was speaking to one familiar with the ways of the fae and this tete a tete suddenly became more amusing.

"He called himself the Enchanter," he responded. She was less than pleased. Merlin had called himself the Enchanter, but the moniker wasn't exclusive to him. She readied herself for

Morc mac Dela's next question, knowing she would have to risk another one after this if she wanted to confirm the Enchanter was indeed Merlin.

He rubbed his hands together, savoring the back and forth. "Now my turn. Who was subject to this justice?"

"Two royal fae houses and one lesser house," she replied without providing specifics. Morc mac Dela relished the morsel nonetheless. Her answer reaffirmed that there were still Fomoire in the Land of Fae as none other could dispense justice to royal houses. Knowing he still wasn't the last of his kind lessened his existential loneliness a measure. "I have another question, if you wish to continue."

"Ask away," he bid her and she could hear the glee in his voice.

"What other knowledge did you share with…" she caught herself as she was about to say "the Enchanter" when she realized that he could have spoken to more than one called the Enchanter. She needed to be more specific, "…this particular Enchanter?" He was silent for some time, but she patiently waited. She knew how much spin she'd put into that curveball.

"I taught him how to place a mortal into a long and peaceful sleep that would only break under preordained circumstances," he reluctantly answered. Try as he might, he could not honestly say less and he felt peeved that his visitor had gotten the better of him.

Bells started ringing in Leader's mind. Infinite Sleep was

one of Merlin's infamous spells, the kernel of truth at the heart of fairy tales like Sleeping Beauty and Snow White. She found it quite ironic, considering it was rumored to be one of the spells used against him when he was imprisoned by Vivian, Mistress of Avalon. If he had never learned it from Morc mac Dela, his fortunes could have played out very differently.

Or not, she corrected herself on second thought. Merlin always had problematic relations with his apprentices and he probably would have found another way to sabotage himself. It took a lot of hubris to manage to get trapped despite having impressive prophetic talents.

"I've answered your question fairly," the Fomoir called out. "Now tell me, what was the crime?"

She said a single word, "Theft." That surprised him. The item taken must have been of some importance for the Fomoire to get involved. "I have one last question for you before I must leave."

"So soon?" he lamented. "We were having such a lovely time."

"All good things must come to an end."

He scoffed at the notion. *She must be mortal. No faerie would say such drivel.* "Go on."

"What was the nature of the knowledge he gave you in exchange for what you shared with him?"

He paused to appreciate a well-chosen question. The answer would illuminate both his interests and the Enchanter's knowledge. In the spirit of the game, he answered as generally as possible. "How to travel through different realms."

She basked in his answer; that was enough to confirm her suspicions about the nature of the Voynich manuscript. *But I'm not finished yet*, she reminded herself to stay focused. She still had to answer one last question, and the ancient Titan did not disappoint. "Who took what from whom?"

Leader shaved away as much detail as possible, but she had to reveal something. There was no hiding behind *technically* answering the question like there was with fiends. She had to respond in the spirit of truth. That was the pact when dealing with faeries. She weighed which part would be the least dangerous to tell the Fomoir and broke the bad news to him. "House Dela took something precious from the heart of fae."

He didn't need to know the particulars of the punishment to know that his clan was no more, so great did the Magh Meall shake with fury. He roared from the other side of the stone, a cry Leader had heard before: the wail of a parent who has lost their child. She stood witness to his grief. Regardless what he wrongs he'd committed, it was only fair.

When he was capable of words, he spoke softly to her. "Thank you for telling me. For your honesty, I'll tell you something without obligation. The Enchanter is not just mortal, but part infernal. They do not honor the spirit of truth." If she'd had any doubts that the Enchanter was Merlin, that disclosure eradicated them. Merlin was the offspring of an incubus and woman.

"Thank you for the warning," she matched his tone. "Goodbye, Morc mac Dela."

"Wait! Can you tell me who you are...in case someone should come asking about you in epochs to come?" he pressed.

She smiled at his cheek and threw him a bone, "I am a friend of fae."

His laughter echoed through his three lightless rooms. "I look forward to our next conversation, friend of fae."

Leader walked away without saying another word. During her visit, the sun had set and the stars were starting to sparkle. On a whim, she whistled and a cadre of fireflies answered the summons, lighting her retreat in phosphorescent beauty. It reminded her of the old days. Once she cleared the mound, she thanked them for their service and dismissed them and they scattered in all directions like a starburst.

For a brief moment, she felt sorry for Morc mac Dela. From stem to stern, all of House Dela was banished from the light of day. There was something tragically poetic about it that resonated with her. *Perhaps it had been written in the stars*, she aphorized philosophically. *No one escapes their fate.*

She cast her mood aside; now was not the time to navel gaze. The Morcandian Key needed to be secured and there was still a missing quire to find. In her hand, she created a bubble and blew it up until it was life-sized. She stepped inside and floated away from the middle lands of the British Isles. She chased the sun until it was just above the horizon. When she popped the bubble, she was back in the mortal realm, more specifically the Salt Mine owned farmland in Sumpter Township, Michigan.

Just beyond the woods, a black SUV was waiting for her. LaSalle exited as soon as he saw her clear the tree line. "David, we need to pick up some food and coffee on the way back to the office," she informed him. "It's going to be a long night."

"Any preference on dinner?" he asked as he opened the door for her.

"Something Chloe and Dot will like," she replied as she slid into the back seat.

As he arranged an order for pickup, she reviewed what she knew. Since she'd not yet read Dot's translation, all she could do was replay what the librarians had told her earlier today. Something Chloe had said in passing took on new meaning: an ink recipe. It was the last thing Merlin had written.

Telepathic written communication was an innate ability of the fae. They didn't need special components, rituals, or spells to accomplish it. They could pick up a stick and leave a message in wet mud if they wanted. But Merlin wasn't fae. In order for him to do it, he would need to lock in his will into something tangible. The magic was in the language metaphorically, but it was *literally* in the ink.

"Food will be ready by the time we get back into town," LaSalle informed her when he was back in the driver's seat.

"Good. We'll also need to prepare a supply drop for Stigma

and Lancer in the field," she added to his to-do list.

LaSalle looked into his rearview mirror and saw the glint in her steely gray eyes. "Yes, Leader."

Chapter Fifteen

From his underground office in the Lubyanka Building, Alexander Lukin worked his way through Konev's report, listing his findings at Schlass Wollef. The captain's conclusion was that the loss of the triad and signet ring were the result of deliberate action by an unknown professional adversary, as evidenced by the way the bodies were disposed. The tendrils of a cruel smile worked away from the corners of his mouth as his blue eyes parsed a significant bullet point: confiscation of all identifying papers and phones before dumping the bodies in the river.

Ah, Misha, you should be more careful! Unfortunately for Konev, Lukin had recovered Lokhov's phone from the Sûre—the mobile he'd witnessed Konev retrieve and throw back into the river. Right now, all the phone proved was that Konev lied in an official report, but Lukin bet what was on the SIM was more damning for the ambitious captain. Otherwise, he would have brought it in and included it in his report.

Never one to tip his hand, Lukin had taken it to a third-party rather than using internal tech because there was less of a chance Volsky or Konev would know it had been brought in if it stayed out of official channels. It should be ready this afternoon, but he suspected he already knew what was on it—proof that Konev had asked the triad to break mission protocol and take possession of a manuscript.

Lukin savored the final point on Konev's report: Given the timing of interception, an internal leak could not be ruled out. His gut felt that this could be the rope upon which both Konev and Volsky hung. It was the sort of thing that was delicate, something one mentioned in private conversation to protect themselves and allow their superior some latitude on how to handle it. In their line of work, intelligence leaks were anathema, and its mere mention invited unwanted attention. By committing it to writing in a filed report, Volsky would be forced to officially address it. *The chairman's going to birth a litter!*

Lukin sat back in his chair and reviewed what he'd learned during his stopover in Sophia, Bulgaria. When offered two green straps of one hundred euro bills, the vulgar bookseller had divulged his client's full history without batting an eye. Lukin had other ways of extracting information, but open purse strings was one of the perks of working a personal mission for the general secretary of the Ivory Tower. In his experience, twenty thousand tax-free euros were enough to loosen almost anyone's lips.

Lukin was honestly puzzled why Konev was so interested in the Voynich material. It wasn't enchanted—the Ivory Tower had checked it out at the Yale library—and it was completely indecipherable. There was no esoteric knowledge to be gained when no one could read the damn thing. If Konev's interest wasn't magical in nature, it had to be monetary. *But what buyer could Konev have that someone like Sebek couldn't rustle up on his own for the full commission?* Lukin argued against himself. On top of his legitimate bookstore, the Bulgarian was running off-books black-market auctions. His net was cast wide.

Lukin went back and forth on how best to use what he knew. His body reflected his indecision as he swiveled side to side in his chair. He leaned back and the old hinges creaked as he put his feet on his desk. He found himself staring at the ceiling, painted sunshine yellow decades ago in one administrator's desperate attempt at improving morale. It didn't: it just clashed with the walls and floor.

He followed the familiar cracks in the paint until he found his ever companion in the far corner: a crackle that looked like a capuchin monkey smoking a cigar. There was nothing whimsical about the face; it looked like a grizzled WWII *starshina* just about to dress down some clueless private fresh out of basic training. It'd amused him the first time he saw it and now his unconscious mind always sought it out when he found himself in this position: at a crossroads with unmarked paths.

"So, Starshina Monkey, it is just you and me again, eh?" he addressed the corner of his ceiling. "What do you think? Is it time to play it safe or take a gamble?" He put his hand up to ear, pantomiming listening.

Starshina Monkey remained silent, but Lukin heard what he wanted to hear and barked out a bitter laugh. "I knew you would say that, you old bastard. Let's drink to it!"

He sat upright and retrieved a near-empty bottle of Killepitsch along with a glass from the bottom left drawer. The dark, fruity liqueur was native to Düsseldorf, and it had been his mother's favorite. It was through her that he'd acquired a taste for it, starting with watered-down sips on special occasions as a child. Some took his preference for a German drink over their beloved vodka as an insult, so he kept it out of sight lest his Russianness come into question, never mind that he was born and raised in Moscow.

After a quick blow, he deemed the glass clean enough and poured in two fingers of the blood red liquid. The first toast was to Starshina Monkey—it would be rude to not toast a true comrade first—and the second was always to his deceased parents. It went down smooth with a sweet finish. He wiped the glass dry with a tissue before putting it and the bottle back into the drawer. It was time to write his report for General Secretary Yastrzhembsky.

The main takeaway was informing Yastrzhembsky of suspected Salt Mine involvement and alerting him to Konev's divided attention, but the devil was in the details. Lukin started with listing what actually happened before making editorial adjustments. He found creative deviations that were close to the truth where easier to believe and defend. With the factual information down, he selectively trimmed parts and changed others.

First, he left out the phone recovery, both by Konev and himself; including it would only lead to increased scrutiny about things to come. Next, he created a fictional tail that was following Konev and supported it with some photos. The first was taken in the wooded area along the Sûre River shortly after Konev finished his ritual. Within the blurry dark was a constellation of shadows that looked remarkably like a third party in hiding. The second picture was a clearer image of someone he'd photographed off the street: a shifty-looking French tourist whom he'd previously asked for directions. Both images were genuine and unaltered, and there wouldn't be anything to be found on follow-up, should someone bother.

He reported finding and destroying two bugs commonly used by Western agencies in Konev's room after the captain had left for his return flight to Moscow, which was a half-truth because Lukin did reenter the hotel room but only to destroy the bugs that he'd planted. Sebek's part he left intact as well as the information about the container landing in Saint Petersburg next week. Then, he tied a bow around the whole lie: Konev was a man deeply into his side-earning private affairs who had attracted attention from either Western powers or aggravated private actors. *These forces may or may not be responsible for intercepting the triad and primary objective*, Lukin dictated his final sentence in his head while he typed. It was the kind of assertion that didn't need to be verified to cast a shadow of a doubt over Konev's character. It said nothing and it said everything, and it was perfect.

He reread his narrative from the beginning, making sure it held water and fixing grammar and typos along the way. After a few substitutions in word choice to establish the right tone, it was ready. He sent the report directly to Yastrzhembsky and declared to Starshina Monkey, "*Alea iacta est.*"

He turned off the light and locked his door behind him before striding down the long corridor to the bank of elevators. He summoned a carriage by pressing the down button. The bottom level of the Lubyanka Building was wryly referred to as "the basement" and it was the domain of the Ivory Tower's imp network.

Imps were one of the lowliest types of devils and the least evil of the bunch. They were rarely outright villainous, leaning toward pettiness or mischievousness over cruelty, which left them on the periphery of proper fiendish society. Imps had a knack for picking up bits of information because they were often ignored or overlooked in Hell. Their social cachet was measured against each other in a continual bargaining for position, information, and favors.

The Tower had started using imps under the suggestion of Lukin's parents. As inherently magical beings, they had access to knowledge beyond the mortal realm, and as marginalized members of Hell's legions, they were easy to recruit. Imps were often bound into service of loftier devils who had the ability to mark them for destruction for even the smallest of infractions; it wasn't hard to entice them.

The Interior Council offered to "liberate" imps that were marked for destruction in exchange for service to the Tower. If an imp agreed to the terms, the Tower brought them to the mortal realm and bound them by the neck with an ivory collar which hid them from scrying provided they remained within the Tower's complex. Superficially, it appeared just another form of servitude, but being a slave was better than annihilation and the Russians were less difficult to work for than their previous masters.

The potential of an imp network was fully realized as their ranks grew. Individual imps were limited in what they knew, but they held fast to clannish structures, which meant every imp—and what they knew—was connected to every other imp in one way or another. With enough numbers, time and bribes, the wily little devils could ferret out most secrets from the nooks and crannies of Hell all the while the proper fiends remained oblivious to their presence.

Over time, the imps became essential as the Ivory Tower found new ways to exploit their natural abilities. With their prodigious memory, imps replaced the endless banks of filing cabinets when the Tower decided to go paperless for security purposes. Their ability to convey information by direct neural transmission became the preferred method of briefing an operative in a hurry. Even though they were relegated to the basement, they had a measure of regard in the Tower that they'd never had in Hell. And although the food and entertainment in the mortal realm was definitely better than Hell's, it was the sense of being important that they most appreciated.

Lukin's destination was the very first imp the tower had employed, one Mr. Grizel Greedigut. Greedigut had been hand-chosen by his parents in the early days of the Tower. The tiny imp was only a foot tall and kept his horns short and his beard long, partly covering his pendulous pot belly. He was extremely fond of food, tobacco, and pornography, and his personal Hell would be having to choose which one of the three to forgo. His mottled skin varied between burgundy and imperial red and his eyes were solid black like a great white shark's. Lukin had spent more time than he liked peering into those bottomless pits during information transfers.

Lukin rounded several corners, ignoring the normal hoots, howls, and yammering that filled the basement at all hours. Imps had a reputation among fiends of being quiet and unobtrusive, but the Tower had found that they ceased being so when the threat of destruction no longer hung over their heads. When he arrived at Greedigut's office, he found the door closed, which was odd. The imp liked to live life out loud for everyone to hear.

He pressed his ear to the door but heard nothing. Then, he knocked. "Griz, you inside?"

The din of several things falling onto the concrete floor came from within, and Lukin heard Greedigut cursing over the crash. "Goddammit, Sasha! Give an imp some warning, why don't you?" he yelled from the other side of the door.

Lukin wasn't sure exactly *how* he should have given more warning than a knock on a closed door, but he took it as permission to enter. As he opened the door, he got an unenviable view of the plump and naked backside of its occupant, who was bending over to retrieve a pile of fallen cassette tapes. The imp swayed his rump lasciviously and blew him a kiss over his shoulder. "Take a picture, it'll last longer." His voice was entirely too deep to come from such a small creature, which only made the scene more disturbing.

Lukin adverted his eyes, but it was too late. He could not unsee what had been seen. "You want help with that?"

"No, sit down and try not to destroy anything else, you big oaf," Greedigut chastised him grabbing the tapes five at a time in each hand. Lukin was only five foot ten, but he took Greedigut's point—the small office was significantly more cramped once he was inside.

Lukin took a seat on the other side of the desk while the imp flew up and down, stacking the tapes next to the old

Panasonic cassette player on his normal-sized desk. It took three trips before they were all back in place, and Lukin couldn't help himself. He took a peak at the titles.

"*Avtomaticheskie udovletvoriteli*? Punk *magnitizdat*? You're listening to bootleg '80's Soviet punk music now?" he asked incredulously.

"It's better than whatever crap you like," the imp said defensively as he turned the spines away from Lukin.

"I'm sure Stravinsky's rolling in his grave over your criticism," Lukin slathered the sarcasm thick.

"Whatever. At least this stuff has emotion," Greedigut argued as he took a seat in the tall chair he'd carved for himself. Its purpose was to let him work at the desk despite his small stature, but the imp had taken it upon himself to give it some style. It was a ridiculous little throne with flowing dragon ornamentations in the back and a gaudy purple and gold velvet seat cushion, adding an extra "P" to imp.

"True, true," Lukin drily agreed. "*The Rite of Spring* is famous for its lack of feeling."

Hating being outmaneuvered, the imp bluntly asked, "Whaddaya you want?"

Lukin tipped his head to the side. "A favor."

At first, Greedigut thought Lukin was messing with him— Lukin didn't like to be in anyone's debt—but as soon as he saw he was serious, the imp laid into him. "You come into my house, insult my music, and then ask for a favor? The balls on you!"

"I never insulted your music. It does that well enough on its own. No need for my assistance," Lukin said with a smirk as he called the imp's bluff. He knew Greedigut would be too curious to say no.

The imp's black orbs zoomed in on him and Lukin broke eye contact before he could make a connection. Instead of anger, Greedigut laughed. "Okay, Sasha, I'll bite. What's up?"

"I'd like you to nose around the network to see what Captain Mikhail Timofeiovich Konev has been researching, off the books."

Greedigut tried to read Lukin's face, but it was impassive. He fished for more information. "Asking me to snoop on another agent? That's a big favor on the other side of respectable imp behavior."

"That's why I came to you, Griz. There's no one in the basement that's better at discretion," Lukin replied.

The flattery was apparent, but the imp didn't think it dishonest. He prided himself on always getting more information than he gave. As far as imps go, he considered himself a tight-lipped sonofabitch. "What's in it for me?"

"What do would you need?" Lukin answered his question with a question.

"Well, first and foremost, coverage from blowback." Ivory Tower's politics were not nearly as brutal as Hell's, but if he was going to hang his ruby butt out on a limb, he was certainly going to cover that ass.

"That sounds reasonable," Lukin replied evenly.

"In writing," Greedigut pressed. Every imp was used to doing some nosing that wasn't quite official, but snooping into the activities of a field agent for another agent was the kind of thing that could spiral out of hand quickly. There could be serious consequences and he wanted something that would put the full blame onto Lukin if he was caught.

"I can provide that," Lukin said without hesitation.

Greedigut did a double take. "That was awful quick, boss. Makes me think this goes higher up that you." Lukin restrained a smile. The imp was always a sharp one.

"Griz, you know I wouldn't expose myself for someone as trivial as him," Lukin answered obliquely.

"I know of a fist fight that says otherwise," the imp snidely remarked.

Lukin waved his hand. "Occupational hazard."

"You broke his nose at a party."

"It was a work party," Lukin corrected him. "These things happen when people have drunk too much vodka at office socials."

"If you say so. I wouldn't know. We're not invited to those things." Sensing deeper pockets, Greedigut rattled off a list of his current desires. "If someone else is funding this, I want a new computer with a massive hard drive, a dual cassette player, two tins of McClelland Frog Morton tobacco, a month's worth of food deliveries, and a liter of Miau chocolate milk every day until the end of the year."

"Done!" Lukin exclaimed and held out his hand before the imp lived up to his name and added more demands.

The portly devil rose and shook the man's hand. "Am I looking for anything in particular?"

"Anything not related to a case in the past three years and anything to do with old manuscripts or books," Lukin gave the imp parameters.

Greedigut gave him a toothy grin. "Leave it to me, Sasha."

Chapter Sixteen

Martinez considered herself in shape. She ran. She lifted weights. She stretched and foam rolled. She'd participated in plenty of fitness challenges and dabbled in whatever was the craze of the day. So when Haddock suggested renting bikes to find a suitable place to cross into the Magh Meall, she didn't bat an eye.

What she hadn't anticipated was how sore her butt would be. She'd spent her childhood on a bike but quickly abandoned it as soon as she got her driver's license, and this excursion involved a lot more sitting and was definitely longer than the run-of-the-mill spin class. The saving grace was how incredibly flat the terrain was and the quality of the bike paths. They were in better shape than some roads in the US. She thought Portlanders were serious about cycling, but the Dutch took it to the next level.

She pedaled after Haddock, who was riding point looking for a place to break from the path that was sufficiently secluded, which was proving surprisingly difficult. The nature reserve wasn't packed like the cities, but the Netherlands was a country of seventeen million people crammed into land roughly the size of Vermont and New Hampshire. Finding privacy in a natural space wasn't as easy as would be expected.

Haddock signaled with his arm and Martinez followed as they took a turn at a junction which became a dirt path and eventually grass and mud. The bikes weren't built for off-road, and she thanked her lucky stars that she didn't bite it. Despite their reputation for sensibility, the Dutch didn't wear helmets when they cycled and the man working the bike rental just smirked at her when she asked for one.

Their pace slowed but Haddock took that as a good sign. Paths meant regular travel, and they needed somewhere where they wouldn't be disturbed for at least an hour or two. He hopped off his bike and walked to a patch of tall grass where they could operate in relative obscurity.

"What do you think?" he asked Martinez for her opinion.

"I think I should have gotten bike shorts," she muttered as she did a 360. "Probably as good as we're going to get."

Haddock checked the time. "We'd better get started."

Martinez called dibs. "I'll set up the inside if you dig the circle."

Haddock grabbed the trenching tool and got to work while Martinez unpacked lunch, the ritual accoutrements, and the equipment LaSalle had sent them. The pair had been tasked to retrieve items from the Dimwash, the Magh Meall corollary to the Bourtange Moor. The fact that Haddock recently relieved the estate of Hendrik van der Meer of a series of books on the Dimwash did not escape notice, but the information in the books certainly made their job that much easier. Chloe and Dot were able to give them detailed information and descriptions of what they were looking for.

At one time, the whole region was bog—not to be confused with a march, swamp, or fen as she'd learned while looking up the terrain online—but after centuries of harvesting peat and draining land for agriculture and development, the reserve in southeast Drenthe was all that was left of the Dutch portion of the bog.

Martinez consulted the compass and placed a lit candle on all four cardinal directions. When Haddock had finished digging out the circle, she lined it with crumbled *speculaas*, a spiced Dutch shortbread that was pressed and cut into windmills. They devoured the sandwiches and drank tons of water. Once they entered the Magh Meall, there would be no eating, but Weber had sent them the grounded canteen in case they had to stay longer than anticipated.

Martinez made sure the canteen was filled to the brim before they began their hour of meditation. They sat opposite each other, intertwining their will into a rope and coiling it into a metaphysical sphere around them. When the clock ticked over to thirteen, they crossed into the middle lands.

As always, the first thing they noticed was the smell,

although it wasn't the clean crisp air Martinez had come to associate with the Magh Meall. It was the earthy perfume of ancient moss, and she suddenly found herself craving Scotch. She opened her eyes and saw low shrubs, moss, and pools of water in the purple-tinged light instead of towering trees. The earth under her was sound, but also felt soft and spongy.

"This is different," she commented. "Where should we start?"

"Let's start with the easy one," he suggested. "I'll get the six inch cube of moss if you set the dragonfly trap." He grabbed the trenching tool and stepped outside the circle. Bogs were mostly peat, formed by layers of slowly decaying plant material in fresh water. While the soil was poor in nutrients, the resulting peat was carbon dense and made for good insulation or fuel when burned.

While he dug, Martinez grabbed the bottle of orange blossom honey and stepped ten paces from the circle in the opposite direction. She piled a generous golden ribbon on a patch of dry ground. Everything loved honey, but hawk-eyed dragonflies were particularly fond of it. Their keen sense of smell would pick it up miles away.

Haddock was already bagging the chunk of soil when she returned the honey and pulled out her collapsible fishing rod. She handed him a net and a jar. "Let's let the honey do its thing while we go frog hunting."

The terrain was flat, but geography did not follow the same

rules in the middle lands, and they anchored a guideline in the center of the circle before venturing out. They were in search of a fragrant herb with clubbed leaves that flowered small canary yellow blooms when it bolted. According to the Dimwash guides, it was found along water and attracted the favored insect snack of amethyst-speckled frogs.

They stopped when they found a suitable pool with patches of the licorice-scented herb growing on the banks. Martinez quickly assembled her rod and line and remembered something her father used to say. "You never know when you'll have the time and want to do a little fishing." It brought a smile to her lips. *If only you knew what I was fishing for today, Dad.*

"Isn't fishing for frogs cheating?" Haddock questioned her sportsmanship.

She extended her arm to the pool. "If you want to get in that water and do it the old-fashioned way, be my guest." There were many ways of catching frogs, but she preferred a colorful lure on a hook over gigging or going bare-hands because it kept her on dry land.

He considered the stagnant pool. In the Magh Meall, things were the absolute paragon of their mortal realm corollaries. This was the boggiest of bogs and the water in that pool was filled by rain that slowly evaporated away to make more peat. He shrugged and raised the net as a show of support. "Let's try it your way."

With a sharp hook, a plastic worm, and a taut line, she

pulled in frog after frog, but that wasn't the trick part. They were supposed to bring back five drams of amethyst-speckled frog urine. Finding an amethyst-speckled frog among the myriad of species was a challenge in and of itself, and neither of them had any idea how to get a frog to urinate or how many frogs it would take to collect two tablespoons of urine.

The net came in handy when they caught something other than an amethyst-speckled frog and had to toss it back, but it was more of a hindrance than help when they caught one. Frogs were slippery buggers and if any of their legs made contact with Haddock's hand while he tried to get them out of the net, they made a jump for it every time.

When Martinez suggested grabbing their backs after she pulled them out of the water, it seemed to work better, but he learned the hard way not to face the frog while doing it. The clear stream wasn't particularly smelly, but something deep in his soul indignantly knew it was urine. Martinez kept hold of the line but couldn't stop laughing.

"Well, I can cross getting peed on in the Magh Meall off my bucket list," he joked.

She looked for the silver lining between her giggles. "At least we know it's not hard to get a frog to pee."

"This poor guy is spent," he lamented as he took the frog off the hook and placed it on the ground. The deep purple amphibian with dark blue and black spots leaped frantically for the pool. "Don't warn your friends about us!" he cautioned it.

Through trial and error, they perfected what he called "the dangle and tickle." Martinez would pull the frog out of the water and he would grab its spine from behind. If it didn't pee straight away, he would stroke its exposed belly with the rim of the jar. When the frog inevitably tried to defend itself, he slipped the container under the stream and captured the precious fluid. Then, he took the frog off the hook and let it leap to freedom.

"For such small creatures, they sure pee a lot. They must be something like ten percent pee by weight. Maybe twenty," he exaggerated as he tapped the jar. "Shall we see if we have enough?"

Martinez pulled a glass vial from a foam-lined box, a small funnel, and a fine mesh tea strainer from her backpack. "There's only one way to find out."

The strainer fit in the top of the funnel, which she held over the vial while he carefully poured the urine from the jar. The runes carved into the glass became visible against the pale liquid and she gladly topped it with a rubber stopper. "Looks like your frog tickling days are over."

Martinez put everything back in her bag and collapsed her rod while he emptied the jar and rinsed it out in the pond water, figuring it couldn't be dirtier than urine.

"Two down and one to go," he mentally ticked off another item on their Dimwash list. "Let's go see if the dragonflies have found the honey."

They followed their guideline back to the circle and found a hive of activity hovering above the mound of honey. Their pale blue bodies glinted in the midday sun like rods of glass as heir intricately patterned iridescent wings fluttered double time. It was a feeding frenzy as they drove in and battled for a sweet morsel with their darting tongues. Haddock immediately dropped the net over the cluster of dragonflies before they could scatter.

"You're such pretty little things. It's a shame you must die," he menaced like an original Bond villain.

Martinez pulled out a sack of cotton balls and a small bottle of acetone-free nail polish remover. "How many of these do you think we'll need?"

He shrugged. "How fast do you want to them die?"

"I suppose it isn't really something you can overdo," she concurred as she started tossing saturated cotton balls in the jar. She stopped at five, figuring there should be enough ethyl acetate inside if she was starting to get bothered by the sweet acrid smell. "Toss them in."

He twisted the opening of the net shut before lifting it off the ground and putting them inside. Martinez covered the jar and grabbed her phone to check the time out of habit.

"Damn it," she cursed as she put it away. Not only did her mobile not have coverage, but time passed differently in the Magh Meall. It eluded mortal measurement.

"Take a seat and relax. I'll tell you a story and we'll check at the end," Haddock suggested. Martinez agreed—it was better than counting Mississippis.

"What tale of daring do will you recount for me?" she poetically inquired as she settled in for one of his performances. Haddock was a natural born storyteller with an endless supply of yarns.

"Well, considering our location, how about the tale of Walewein. Technically he's a Flemish hero, but his account is written in Middle Dutch, so I'm going to count it."

She nodded thoughtfully as if all that made sense. "And who, pray tell, is Walewein?"

"Walewein is the nephew of King Arthur."

Martinez dubiously stated, "I don't remember him from any of the King Arthur stories."

"There are plenty of medieval romances that borrowed characters and ideas from the Arthurian tradition but didn't make it into what's considered the modern canon. Some of the French stuff was quite racy. Think of this as fourteenth century Dutch fan fiction," he explained before chiding her. "Now do you want to hear about Walewein?"

"Yes please," she apologized.

He started his story as all good fairytales do. "Once upon a time in a kingdom far, far away, King Arthur held court in Camelot. As was customary, there was much feasting, drinking, music, and dance. However, the revelry came to a halt when a beautiful chessboard floated inside. Decorated in gold and ivory and inlaid with precious stones, it immediately captured the king's fancy at first sight. Arthur knew he had to have it, but the elusive chessboard took off as suddenly as it appeared.

"When he asked which of his knights wished to retrieve it for their king, none stepped forward. He asked again, this time promising all his land and the throne after his death, but no one dared to follow it. It smacked of sorcery. When a furious and inebriated Arthur vowed to chase it down himself, one knight was so ashamed by his king's valor and his own initial cowardice that he stepped forward."

"Walewein," Martinez answered as if this was a panto.

"Exactly. Walewein leapt upon his trusty steed Gringolet and pursued the chessboard through the treacherous woods. When it slid through a crack in a mountain, Walewein widened the entrance with his bare hands and slew the dragons that resided there. When it crossed a rushing river, he dove in and clawed his way up the opposite bank. Walewein gave it no quarter and the hounded chessboard took refuge in the castle of King Wonder."

"Best wrestler name ever," Martinez chirped an aside.

"King Wonder was a crafty ruler. He knew opportunity when he saw it and struck a bargain. He agreed to give Walewein the chessboard if he brought him the sword with two rings held by the formidable King Amoraen in Castle Ravensteen. What King Wonder didn't tell him was that it was far away and the path dangerous."

Haddock paused and Martinez took that as a cue for some impromptu dramatic music. "Dun, dun, dun!"

"On the road, Walewein met a traveler on his way to be knighted by King Arthur so that he might issue a challenge to the man who killed his brother. Unfortunately, he had been robbed en route and only had the clothes on his back and his thin nag. Walewein took pity on the squire and agreed to help him by defeating the robber baron that stole his possessions, giving him his own horse, and helping him get knighted to avenge his brother's death."

"Umhm," she hummed an accusation. "Someone's avoiding their quest."

"He wouldn't be very chivalric if he didn't help," Haddock said in Walewein's defense before continuing the story. "Eventually, Walewein made it to Castle Ravensteen, and King Amoraen agreed to give him the sword with two rings on one condition—that Walewein should travel to India and use the sword to bring back the beautiful daughter of King Assentine to be his bride."

Martinez tisked and shook her head. "Yet another story that doesn't hold up in the modern age."

Given her stated disdain with the final part of the threefold quest, he chose to skip the encounter with the Red Knight that involved assault and battery of a fair maiden and Walewein pushing her to forgive her abuser. Every narrator took dramatic license and Haddock could tell that "He's really sorry, think about the fate of his soul!?" wasn't going to be received well.

"Her name was Ysabele, and she was King Assentine's pride and joy. She roamed the beautiful gardens on her father's estate which was surrounded by twelve walls, each guarded by eighty knights. But Walewein was not daunted. Wielding the sword with two rings, he cut down hundreds of knights before getting an audience with King Assentine.

"Exhausted by all the fighting he'd done just to get inside the castle, Walewein was overpowered by King Assentine, who was a strong and able fighter in his own right. But before he could kill Walewein, his daughter, the lovely Ysabele, requested to meet the knight before his execution. King Assentine could refuse his daughter little and therefore agreed, but much to his dismay, Ysabele fell for Walewein and he for her peerless charms. King Assentine tried to separate the lovers, but they escaped and fled his domain, beset by thieves and thugs but aided by friends past."

"Oh, this isn't going to end well. He's got to give up the girl—a knight's word is his bond," Martinez insisted.

"Which was why the pair were overjoyed to discover King Amoraen had died during their harrowing journey back from India," he skipped over the twists and turns of their return.

"And he gives the sword to King Wonder and the chess set to Arthur and they all lived happily ever after," Martinez cut to the chase.

"Well, there are more side quests and ancillary characters.

There's a magical fox that's actually a cursed man, and Ysabele gets kidnapped—"

Martinez rolled her eyes. "Of course she does."

"But Walewein gets her back and eventually his horse as well, but that is the gist of it," he confirmed. It was anticlimactic as far as endings go for an Arthurian story, but he could tell he was losing his audience. Martinez wasn't the sort for a convoluted medieval story, unlike the three ghosts that lived in her house.

She motioned to the covered jar. "Let's see how the dragonflies are faring." He held the net as she removed the lid, but nothing fluttered. "I guess it worked."

Haddock separated individual insects from the net while Martinez carefully removed their wings with tweezers. She didn't relish the task, but the wings were what Chloe and Dot asked for and as the designated carrier, she had no interest in increasing the karmic load by carrying anything unnecessary. Everything they had collected was pretty mundane—nothing as significant as the waters of Narcissus—but bringing anything native to the Magh Meall home with them had a cost.

She carefully counted the wings as she put them in a padded container and secured it in her bag. "What's left?"

Haddock consulted the list, "Sea grass and sand from the bottom of the Zuiderzee and a fungus that only grows on dead Dutch gnomes."

"Strangest scavenger hunt ever," she declared. "But no

more cycling fieldtrips after this, right?" she checked on behalf of her butt.

He laughed. "No."

"Then let's go back and get a shower and a hot meal," she suggested. The sandwiches felt like hours ago and breakfast had only been sliced bread with assorted cold cuts and cheese.

They brought all their gear into the circle and focused their will on home. As soon as they were back, Martinez got on her phone and made a donation to even her karmic slate. She was never one to press her luck if she didn't have to.

They collected their bikes and walked through the tall grass toward the path. "A blinged-out floating chess board I can imagine, but what the hell does a sword with two rings look like?" she wondered.

"Rings are the discs of metal on either end of the sword's handle. They helped counterbalance the weight of large blades," he answered academically.

"So, it's basically a sword...?"

"Yes, a heavy sword that was easy to wield in a fight. *The Roman van Walewein* was written over 600 years ago so that was cutting-edge tech at the time."

Martinez groaned at his pun. "I mean this in the nicest way possible, but you are such a dork."

Chapter Seventeen

The Zuiderzee was a broad, shallow bay of the North Sea along the Dutch coast. At its deepest, it was only fifteen feet from the surface. For a strong swimmer like Haddock, a pair of flippers and a snorkel would allow him to dive down to collect sand from the bottom and harvest sea grass. He'd need a thick wet suit—the water was chilly even in summer—but that wasn't nearly as difficult to obtain or transport as scuba gear. On paper, it sounded like an easy retrieval.

Unfortunately, the Zuiderzee had all but disappeared in the past hundred years. When the Dutch built the Afsluitdijk in the 1930s, the massive dam separated the Zuiderzee from the North Sea. They drained the water and the reclaimed land became Flevoland, the newest province of the Netherlands. Over time, what water remained became freshwater lakes as they pumped out saltwater and rainwater topped them off.

That left the agents two options: try to get a boat to take them to what was left of the Zuiderzee outside of the dam or cross over to the Magh Meall and bank that it hadn't caught up to the recent man-made changes. To the fae, a century was a blink of an eye.

Booking a ground floor room at a seaside hotel was much easier than chartering a boat, which was why Martinez and Haddock were indoors sitting inside an inflatable raft in wetsuits. The lit candles were placed in cup holders at the cardinal directions and crumbled shortbread circled the raft.

"This is either genius or a terrible idea," Martinez said equivocally.

Haddock grinned as he checked his safety line and his knife. Because he couldn't pull out any of his tattoos while wearing the wetsuit, it would be the only weapon he could access in the water. "Relax. Chloe and Dot seemed to think it was feasible."

"*Feasible* isn't exactly a rousing endorsement," she replied as she secured her holstered Glock around her waist. The alarm clock on the nightstand was minutes away from noon. "It's showtime."

They started the incantation and at the stroke of noon, they entered into meditation and wound their will into a sphere. Theoretically, it would take the entire raft into the Magh Meall where they should land on water. From there, Haddock would retrieve the items and Martinez would stay on the raft, reinforcing the circle in the fluid terrain. If it looked like the circle wouldn't hold, she was supposed to give three sharp tugs on the line, which was Haddock's cue to swim like hell for the raft.

It wasn't difficult to tell when thirteen o'clock had come. The ground beneath them went lax and started undulating. The air turned salty and a forceful breeze whipped across their faces. When they opened their eyes, they were surrounded by water but there was visible land at the edge of the horizon. A school of fish near the surface scattered at their sudden arrival but regrouped once they ascertained the raft didn't look like any predator they had encountered before.

Hail Mary, full of grace... Martinez continued to stream her will around the circle. She generally found performing magic much easier in the middle lands, but she held the rosary Weber had made her in her hand just in case she needed a boost. Trying to maintain a rigid sphere in waves was like trying to keep one's footing in a bouncy castle when everyone around was jumping at different times. It required balance, proprioception, situational awareness, and a good sense of kinetic cause and effect—but you know, metaphysically.

After a few over and under corrections, she found her equilibrium and dropped anchor, metaphorically speaking. When she was certain her will was solid and unyielding, she gave Haddock the signal. "Make it quick," she advised him.

"I'll be back in two shakes of a lamb's tail," he assured her before slipping into the water. Even through his wetsuit, it felt silky against his body. He'd spent much of his adult life in or near water, but he'd never swam in something so luxurious.

He surveyed the aquatic landscape using his snorkel,

watching the explosion of sea creatures scurry away from his large shadow. Their color and shapes were fantastical, more akin to a Caribbean reef than a murky tidal bay of the North Sea. He couldn't even imagine the splendor of Magh Meall's coral reefs. He absently wondered if the purple light caused species to develop different coloration here or if such scientific principles had any influence on enchanted places.

He kept his flippers as still as possible, letting the silt settle to improve visibility. Fortunately, he didn't need fine detail. The general lay of the terrain would do. As the water cleared, he spotted a meadow of verdant fronds drifting in the direction of the current.

He swam for it, staying close to the surface. The last thing he wanted was to get entangled in the vegetation. He took a deep breath before diving down, grabbing the green tops with one hand. With the other, he unsheathed his knife and sliced through the taut sea grass.

He had plenty of breath left in his lungs, but he surfaced anyway, blowing out hard through the snorkel to clear any water before taking a breath in. One wasn't supposed to eat or drink anything in the Magh Meall, and he would feel colossally dumb if he got trapped in the middle lands for accidentally snorting some seawater.

He swam back to the raft and threw the sea grass inside. Under the noonday sun, the satiny fronds glistened. Neither he nor Martinez bothered with containment; that could wait until they were back on terra firma. While he sheathed the knife and grabbed a hard plastic cup, she kept a firm grip on her rosary and pulled the excess rope back inside the raft with the other hand—their warning system only worked if the line was taut.

Haddock took another deep breath and dove straight for the bottom. His flippers flapped furiously to defy his buoyancy. When he was within arm's length of the bottom, he scooped up as much sand as he could with his cup. When he breached the surface, he tossed the cup and his snorkel next to the sea grass.

"I'm coming aboard," he warned Martinez and she nodded, applying counterweight to keep the sphere and circle intact. After he was inside, he pulled all of the rope back into the raft. "Let's get out of here."

With a snap of willful intent, the brisk briny air stilled and went stale and the raft rigid. They were back in their hotel room. The water along the bottom of the raft seeped into the floor and saturated the crumbs of the shortbread.

"I believe that is proof positive that I'm a genius," Haddock crowed.

Martinez shook her head in disbelief. "I can't believe that worked. And all this was underwater less than a hundred years ago."

He reached for his phone on the bed and electronically dropped a donation. "That's what the Dutch do best—reclaim land from the sea. As the saying goes, 'God created the world, but the Dutch created Holland.'" He grabbed his pile of clothes and went to the bathroom to change, leaving Martinez to change beside the raft. Her wetsuit was only barely damp from the incidental water that got into the raft and therefore significantly easier to get off.

"I also can't believe Flevoland is the name of a real place. I would have pegged it as something in the Magh Meall—the mythical home of Guy Fieri," she jested.

"You're thinking of Flavor Town," he corrected her while he peeled off his wetsuit. He vigorous toweled off, in part to bring warmth back into his body, before putting on dry clothes. "My money is the final resting place of rappers who wear giant clocks. Tell me Flava Flav isn't magic: I dare ya."

She smiled as she recalled him dancing on one leg to ABBA in her kitchen. "I never would have pegged you as a hip hop enthusiast."

He dramatically burst through the bathroom door with his best impersonation of a hype man. "Yeah, boyeeeeee!"

Martinez gave him a pity laugh while she shook her head at the sad spectacle. "As a person of color, I'm going to let you off with a warning this time, but don't do that again."

She put the sea grass and sand away with the other components while Haddock deflated the raft. They had their sitting area back but it was soaking wet. He made an attempt at damage control with the towels from the bathroom, but his water control skills were not up to the Dutch standard.

Martinez sighed. "What are we going to do about this?"

He moved the wet towels around with his bare feet. "Call room service and ask for more towels?" He was only half joking.

"Or we pack up and leave for the next location?" she suggested.

Haddock's jaw dropped. "Teresa?!"

"What?" she said defensively before explaining herself. "You know work will cover the charges, it would save us the hassle of making up a reasonable explanation for the mess, and we wouldn't have to stay in a soggy room."

"I'm not saying your idea isn't good. I'm just surprised you suggested it before I did. You're supposed to be the responsible one in this duo," he teased.

She smirked as she started packing up their things. "Ever consider that you're a bad influence?"

He feigned shock and clutched his proverbial pearls. "I'll have you know I only use my powers for awesome."

Chapter Eighteen

Martinez stood under her umbrella in front of the giant gnome statue, re-reading the placard to make sure she had a handle on the situation. She had a hard time deciding what was most ridiculous: the inspiration for the Smurfs was real, their King Kyrië was killed by a hunter in the winter of 1951-52—possibly '52 to '53, there was room for debate—or that the Dutch rebuilt the dead king's tumulus after clearing it for land development in order to turn it into a pilgrimage site.

Technically, the giant stone figure wasn't a gnome, but a *kabouter*, which was somewhere between a gnome or leprechaun in local mythology. They were helpful, shy little creatures that lived in forests, hills, underground passages, and sometimes in mushrooms. The famous Dutch wooden shoes were supposedly an invention taught to a carpenter by a grateful kabouter, which the statue wore along with a pointy hat and pipe in hand.

The Campine region was historically kabouter territory and said to be where King Kyrië was buried. The problem was that there were many tumuli in the area, some dating back to the bronze age, and the one popularly regarded as King Kyrië's was a recreation.

"Who knew getting frog urine was going to be the easy part?" she drily muttered to Haddock, who stood beside her.

"We just have to get creative," he said optimistically. "How about we get inside, grab a snack and something warm to drink?" It had been raining off and on all morning, and the dark overcast sky suggested it wasn't going to stop anytime soon. Martinez nodded—it wasn't like the stoic statue of King Kyrië was going to give them any clues.

The village of Hoogeloon was amidst all the tumuli and excavated Roman settlements, and local businesses welcomed the attractions as a source of tourist income. Among the string of quaint shops, they found a cafe with an open table for two inside.

"*Twee cappuccino's, twee worstbroodjes en een spa rood, alsjeblieft*," Haddock ordered for them both. Then he switched to Russian, a language they both knew but not many Dutch would. "Initial ideas?"

"Can we find and ask a kabouter?" she said the first thing off the top of her head. They were said to be helpful and little fae creatures were usually pretty easy to bribe.

"Maybe if they were still around, but they left the area after Kyrië's death," he replied.

"Can we summon something that would know? Another local fae?" She deferred to his local knowledge.

185

"Possibly, but summoning isn't exactly my thing," he confessed. "How about you?"

"Do the guides and my ghost roommates count?" she answered his question rhetorically. "That doesn't really help our access problem." Digging for dead gnome royalty wasn't really an option in either the mortal realm or the Magh Meall, albeit for different reasons.

Haddock approached from a different angle. "Do you think this would be any easier to find in the Magh Meall?"

"If the area is forested and his tomb is considered a holy place, it would show up as a clearing," she sussed out the merit in the idea. "But he was killed in the '50s. If the changes to the Zuiderzee hadn't registered, it stands to reason the tomb wouldn't either."

The pair buttoned their lips and smiled as the waitress brought them their drinks and food on little plates and saucers. Martinez picked up what looked like a breadstick and was surprised to find it warm to the touch. She took a bite and nodded in approval. "This is good."

"It's the local take on a sausage roll," he informed her as he stirred a spoonful of sugar into his coffee. "The native cuisine tends to improve the closer you get to the Belgian border, but don't say that in Holland."

Her brow furrowed in confusion. "But we're in Holland."

"No, we're in the Netherlands. Holland is only two provinces: North Holland and South Holland," he gave her a quick geography lesson. "It's kind of gauche to use Holland when you mean the Netherlands."

"If you keep feeding me these, I'll call it whatever it wants me to," she professed and gobbled the rest of the dough-wrapped sausage. She sipped her cappuccino as he tucked into his and her mood improved considerably.

"It's still out there," she insisted. "If someone else had found King Kyrië, I'm pretty sure his body would be on display for ticket sales."

"Unless it's buried in the Magh Meall," he offered a plausible alternative.

She conceded the point with a nod and circled back to the topic of summoning from earlier. "What if we summoned a creature to retrieve it for us? Something that can dig and travel through the earth."

"I like it, but the only thing I can think of that can travel through the ground is an earth elemental, and they aren't exactly the brightest."

Her midbrain flared with memories of seeing an earth elemental summoned by Chuck the Yooper shaman. Intellectually, she knew there was a gradient of elementals, but its size and raw power had made an impression. Forces of nature could be incredibly savage and she wanted something with a lower consequence of failure.

"You know who would know what to summon and how?" she asked innocently but her tone was undermined by the wicked smile on her lips.

Haddock's expression told her he knew where she was headed. He checked the time and did the time zone math. "He should be up and be getting ready for work. It can't hurt to ask."

She pulled out her phone and sent Wilson a message.

*****

Wilson had agreed to help but with conditions. First, he insisted that Martinez perform the ritual. Neither were great at summoning, but she had an attention to detail whereas Haddock was more improvisational by nature. Second, they had to send pictures of the circle and body art for approval before starting. And lastly, they had to call him after it was over.

After they agreed, he proceeded to send them copious amounts of information, some so basic it was almost insulting, but neither of them complained. True to form, Wilson had selected the perfect creature: Kulgude, the treasure-finding *wurm*.

It was culturally native to the area, able to magically travel through soil and seek out desired items, and not native to the mortal realm, which meant if things got out of hand, a banishment bullet would take care of the problem. They already had most of the things she would need for the summoning, and what they were missing would be available at any grocery store.

They scouted out a shielded place between a cluster of tumuli, but they didn't start until it got dark. The ritual had to take place outside—the circle had to be in dirt continuous to the ground. When Martinez had finished constructing the circle with stone, salt, and chalk, she took a picture and sent it to Wilson, who had notes. After she made the corrections, he gave her the green light to continue.

"How did you ever date him?" Martinez huffed.

Haddock drizzled a ribbon of olive oil into the pulverized sage, oregano, rosemary, and thyme. "There are upsides to being with someone thorough," he said blithely with a crooked grin. "Now strip down and let me paint you."

She took off her jacket and shirt and shivered. The temperature was dropping and she was just in her bra and tank top from the waist up. "Why do I have to be in some state of undress to summon things?" she complained.

"Don't ask me: that's all on you. I'm just here to make you pretty." He applied the herbal paste on her chest, arms and face, consulting his phone to make sure he got the pattern right.

"I smell like Thanksgiving stuffing," Martinez said out of the side of her mouth.

"Well, you look fabulous," he said as he wiped his hands on a towel. He snapped a photo for Wilson and checked his gun and ammunition again while he waited for a reply. Martinez had to focus on the summoning, which meant if things went pear-shaped, he would have to banish it.

His phone buzzed. "Perfect. You ready?"

"Ready as I'll ever be," she replied.

Haddock put his hand on the center of her back, one of the few parts of her that wasn't covered in scrolls and symbols. "I'm going to be over there the whole time. At the first sign of trouble, I won't hesitate to shoot."

As he took position behind the shrubbery and cleared out a hole for a clear shot, Martinez lit the candles and set a single stroopwafel to one side inside the circle. Then, she cleared her mind. She swept away the frustration and cold, the fear and doubt until there was nothing left but her core. She summoned her will in the potential space and joined it with the breath in her chest as she started the supplication.

"Kulgude, mover of the earth, bless this humble petitioner with your presence and accept this offering. I have treasure that must be found," she sang out into the dark night. Her Latin was passable and her pitch was a little flat, but that wasn't what was important when it came to attracting Kulgude. The wurm had two weak spots—pride and sweets—and she was appealing to them both.

Her will carried her thin voice beyond the mortal realm and after the fifth supplication, she felt something enter the circle. The smooth end of a giant earthworm erupted in the center of her circle. She had no idea how long it was since most of it was still in the ground, but its head was the size of a softball.

She called it a head because it had a slit that vaguely suggested a mouth, but it was hardly matched the whimsical drawings in the Sibylline cartoons. Martinez now understood why Wilson was so insistent about clearing the patch of ground meticulously—if the circle had been broken, it would not be bound.

"Who seeks Kulgude?" the wurm addressed her telepathically, leaving the question of its mouth in limbo.

"One who seeks something from the tomb of King Kyrië," she answered out loud for Haddock's benefit.

The wurm bobbed and weaved its head, both to show intrigue and to test the circle. She buffeted the knocks and waited for it to reply. "What treasure do you seek from the esteemed king of the kabouters?"

"I require the yellow and brown mushroom that grows on his body—the one shaped like a cup," she answered and pictured it in her mind before pushing it to the wurm.

"That is a strange treasure," it questioned her judgment. Most mortals were interested in gold, silver, jewels and other shiny baubles.

"Does that mean you cannot find it?" she turned the doubt back on the wurm to needle its pride.

"Kulgude can find any treasure!" it roared before toning it down. "That is, for the right price."

"The first is in the circle, a gesture of good faith." She

dropped the veil of will to reveal an outer ring of stroopwafels and the wurm marveled at her cleverness—a circle within a circle. "I have more. I will give you another for each mushroom cup you bring back intact up to ten," she bargained. The head sniffed at the cookie even though it had no nose to speak of. The sweet caramelized apple syrup sandwiched between thin waffle biscuits called to it, and prospect of ten more was tantalizing.

"Kulgude finds your offering acceptable," it continued to refer to itself in the third person. The slit of Kulgude's end opened wide and swallowed the stroopwafel whole. Then, it disappeared down the hole it had entered.

The tumulus must have been close if the rapidity of its return was any indication. The head popped out of the hole and regurgitated a perfect yellow and brown sac fungus from its slit. "Is this the treasure you seek?" it asked before it bothered to venture for another. It had learned long ago that mortals could be fickle.

Martinez took a good look at it in the candle light. "Yes, I believe it is." She dropped her will, making one cookie available to the wurm. "Your reward." And so it went, one by one until the last stroopwafel went down Kulgude's slit.

"Thank you for your service, great Kulgude," Martinez bid it farewell. The smooth segmented end bowed before disappearing into the earth and she sang the virtues of Kulgude as she severed the connection between their worlds.

As promised, she immediately picked up her phone and

sent Wilson a message—she had just finished her first in-the-field fae summoning and all was well. She was wiping down the green paste and getting dressed as Haddock came out of the bushes. "I don't think I'll ever be able to eat stroopwafel again."

Chapter Nineteen

Leader took a deep breath as she entered her workshop, savoring the smell of things being made. Once upon a time, she'd spent much of her days cooking batches of potions, unguents, elixirs, and balms. These were the pieces of practical magic people sought but didn't want anyone else to know they used. Some of the things she made were not enchanted but an early form of medicine—a precursor to the modern chemist. However, when she applied a little enchantment to the pot, there was few who made better. She'd been taught by a true master.

Alchemy was the craft of making magical concoctions, although the name had later become synonymous with the European obsession of turning lead into gold. There was a precision to it but also intuition, like a great baker who followed the recipe but who also knew when the dough needed a little more flour or when a loaf needed just a few more minutes in the oven. She often thought of it as applied chemistry with the unquantifiable element of will.

Despite the fact that she rarely had time to make things after creating the Salt Mine, she'd had a subterranean workshop installed. She liked to keep her hand in and it was the one place in the Mine that was truly hers. Even the fourth-floor office belonged to Leader and thus demanded a certain aesthetic and function. Here, she was just Penelope, surrounded by her tools and favorite things collected over the years.

Stigma and Lancer had returned to Detroit days ago with the raw components for the Voynich ink, but there was preparatory work that needed to be done before the ink could be made. The sand had to be thoroughly dried, the sea grass roasted over the peat, and the fungus milked of its oil. There were modern devices that could have sped up the process, but many of those required electricity and she'd acquired an array of elemental powered items that did the job just fine.

First, she checked the sea grass strewn over the grill. The fire elemental had kept the peat to just below a smolder, slowly desiccating the vegetation until it was thin and brittle. In a heavy stone mortar and pestle, she worked it into a fine powder with rhythmic strokes that had been ground into her muscle memory.

Then, she picked up a ceramic mortar and pestle and pulverized the fungus into a mash. The pulp was placed inside the inner chamber of her centrifuge, which was powered by a bound air elemental. As the tiny whirlwind picked up speed, the oil spun out through fine holes and collected in an outer chamber.

Next, she needed a cooking vessel. Her go-to was a cauldron—of which she had many in different sizes—but considering the scant volume of material she was working with, she opted for a clay crucible. Historically they were used for melting metals because of their tolerance for high temperatures, but she found them reliable for any recipe that called for even heat.

She measured out the powdered sea grass into the bowl and added the frog's urine, making a thin slurry. With her will, she coaxed the fire elemental in the brazier underneath to give low heat. As the dark liquid slowly started to simmer, she added the fungus oil, creating an oil slick that floated on top.

It needed a good stir, which was where the dragonfly wings came into play, but first she had to apply the enchantment. She started singing a song of making, intertwining her will in the lyrics and notes. Then, she dipped the first of the dragonfly wings and stirred widdershins. The slurry seeped into the lacy wing, drawn up by capillary action and her voice. It outlined the intricate pattern in black before disintegrating it and adding it to the pot. One by one, she stirred in her magic with the dragonfly wings until the oil was fully incorporated. She finished the verse, ended her song, and took the crucible off the fire elemental, who she then commanded to slumber.

As the ink rested, she cleaned up using a duster to which an air elemental was bound. The bristles knocked the dust about and the elemental spun it around, depositing it all into a container she had to periodically empty on the surface. With nothing left to do but wait, she made herself to a cup of tea and took a seat in her rocking chair. Beside it was a basket filled with cleaned and combed raw wool and a niddy-noddy—a piece of oak with a perpendicular rod on each end set in opposition. She grabbed her spindle, and with each drop and wobble of the whorl, it spun the wool into a strand of fine yarn. Every so often, she paused and wrapped the yarn around the ends of the niddy-noddy. When it was a substantial amount, she tied the end around the bundle of yarn, slipped it off the wooden pegs, and twisted it into a skein.

She longed to do another but resisted. The ink was probably cool enough to transfer now, and Dot would be waiting for her. It had taken on a silky texture, and it poured out of the crucible with ease. Once it was safely in a lidded pot covered with runes, she had a fire elemental clean the inside. There was little that couldn't be cleansed with fire if it were hot enough.

With the pot of ink and jar of dried sand stowed in a basket, she left her workshop, magically locked the door behind her, and took the elevator up. When she stepped out of the elevator onto the sixth floor, she was once again Leader.

Chloe and Dot were at their circular desk surrounded by stacks of books. While Stigma and Lancer were collecting ingredients, the librarians were diving into all things Merlin. So much of what was reported about the magician was pure drivel, but one had to comb through it to find the kernels of truth, should any exist.

It didn't help that his biggest claim to literary fame was through his association with King Arthur. Historically, there was a military leader named Arthur who led the defense of the British Isles against Saxon invaders after the Romans had left but before the proper kings of Britain, starting with Alfred. However, the details of Arthur's life and exploits later committed to writing were a Welsh and English fiction, often twisted for political or religious purposes.

Tales of Arthur grew in popularity and with it, the scope of the legends. In the thirteenth and fourteenth century, Western Europe was captivated by idyllic Camelot, the chivalrous knights of the round table, and their epic quests. It sparked indigenous non-English Arthurian romances to be written, only a fraction of which made it into canon and often with editorial changes to match religious mores of the time.

Had Chloe and Dot known at the time, they would have paid more attention to the island and its goings on, but they were primitive places of little interest. That was the problem of living through history—it wasn't always easy in the moment to know who or what was going to be significant.

"How's the reading going?" Leader greeted them.

Chloe sighed, "It's going."

"Is that for me?" Dot asked when she saw the basket in Leader's hand.

"Voynich ink and sand for blotting," Leader replied as she set the pot and jar down in front of the surlier of the sisters. Dot happily closed her book and pulled out her calligraphy set. "Any progress on where the last quire might be?" she asked Chloe.

"The analysts have broadened their search, but still no hits on registered private sales and none of Stigma's other contacts deal much in Voynich paraphernalia. After a little more digging into Hendrik van der Meer, we found out that he'd purchased the twenty-first quire from someone in Shanghai, and the seller of the letterlock was in Ethiopia."

"Rather far flung," Leader saw her point, "but it does support the idea that someone wanted to keep them separate considering the bulk of the manuscript was in Italy for centuries. Could it be in our backyard?" She alluded to the New World.

"Maybe if it has been hiding in plain sight and in circulation like the letterlock or quire twenty-one, but if someone hid it away...unlikely. Especially if it was Merlin doing the hiding," Chloe surmised. "Dot thinks if he stashed it before he was trapped, it might be somewhere in or near the lowlands. All the ink ingredients were from there and she thinks much of the manuscript may have been written there.

"No manuscript author wants to have to travel far for more ink, and inevitably you always run out just before you're finished," Dot interjected after she penned the final letter and threw a handful of sand on the parchment to dry the ink.

"There are a few salt deposits and limestone caves in the general area that are worth checking out," Chloe added. Both were desirable for different reasons: salt because it was magically inert and limestone because it could conduct magic.

"The search should go faster with this," Dot remarked as she lifted the slip of parchment and siphoned the sand back into the jar. "All we need is our human radar." She handed it to Leader.

It wouldn't be hard to convince Stigma to gallivant around Europe but foolhardy to send him alone. She could trust Lancer to cover his back and keep him on task, but she was needed on another case. Sending Stigma with Fulcrum was a terrible idea for lots of reasons and that left only one viable choice: Clover.

Chapter Twenty

The bearded truck driver finished another energy drink and tossed the empty can into a sack along with the others. It had been a long journey from St. Petersburg and he'd driven through the night—first down the M-11 to Tver, then east across the Volga skirting the southern side of the massive peat bogs that once drove industry in the region. It had been nothing but traditional blue-painted houses and barns dotting the countryside for the past hour, and despite being daylight, it had a somnolent effect on him. But according to his GPS, he was close to his destination

The remains of the shuttered sugar beet plantation had seen better days. The fields had reverted to the wild and the barn in the back looked abandoned. He was about to check the coordinates when a flash of light blinked from deep within the lot—headlights.

At least I know I'm in the right place, he thought as he pulled down the gravel road and slowed down. He carefully eyed Captain Mikhail Konev as he waved the truck to enter the old log cabin barn. Despite its distressed exterior, the beams were sound and the barn blessedly dry, which made unloading the twenty-foot shipping container with his lift much easier.

He knew better than to ask questions that were none of his business, like why a closed farm in the middle of nowhere was receiving a shipment, why there were already two similar containers inside, or what was inside this box that justified a rush delivery on a Saturday morning. As soon as Konev signed the papers as Georgi Kolchak, the driver got back in his cab and drove away. Whatever was going on, he didn't want to know. He just drove the truck.

Konev closed the barn door for privacy before grabbing his bolt cutters. Like a child in front of a pile of wrapped birthday gifts, he couldn't wait to tear into it. He moved his light to the container's bolt seal and paused when he saw the zebra-striped plastic protective coating, a sign that St. Petersburg customs had been inside.

My container was searched? He panicked, fearing the worst. He'd heard stories that customs wasn't above confiscating items that struck their fancy. He slid the cutters through the bolt, ripped open the door and breathed a sigh of relief when he saw the front end of the 1957 Mercedes Pagoda. His baby was safe.

Hanging just inside the container doors was a plastic bag holding the container's inventory list and accompanying customs papers. He flipped through the pages but stopped when he saw something circled in red: small shipping box containing loose-leaf manuscript. Next to it was scrawled a single word: Absent.

Absent? What the hell does "absent" mean? Confiscated? Never shipped? His mind spiraled. He opened the trunk and confirmed it wasn't there, then immediately phoned Feliks Sebek. The Bulgarian swore up and down that he'd mailed the package to RBO as directed and resent him the tracking number. A quick check online confirmed the package had been delivered.

Next, Konev called RBO. Arnold Schmidt wasn't in the office, but the receptionist verified that the package was received from Sebek and added to his container as requested. She wouldn't have records on who had accessed the container in transit until Monday, but she could verify that it hadn't been opened on its way to Rotterdam.

Konev brusquely hung up and put his phone away. Someone had stolen from him, but he didn't have time to figure out who it was or track down his property. He was supposed to deliver the package to Glumra, the troll scholar of Duncith. Tomorrow. The crusty hulk wasn't going to be pleased; the troll had paid him an advance on the finder's fee to help with Konev's cash-flow issue, which meant he probably had a buyer already lined up. It certainly wasn't out of the kindness of his heart.

He paced the barn and contemplated what to do next. Obviously, he was going to return the advance and profusely apologize but would that be enough? He didn't want to jeopardize future advances as they sometimes exceeded the price Konev paid for the item, and it was all gravy when it was stolen property.

The idea of giving Glumra more money crossed his mind, but it would be insulting, like a child tossing coins at his parents. It was never good to get on the bad side of a troll, particularly one as nasty and vindictive as Glumra. Plus, it could be construed as a bribe and Konev didn't want to get in legal trouble in Duncith. Not that such was likely, but he didn't put anything past Glumra.

A gift! his mind shouted at him. *A token to smooth over this unfortunate turn of events.* He looked around the open container for something Glumra would want, but came up blank. He checked the second container, which housed a 1970 Lotus Elan the color of a robin's egg. *If only he was into sports cars,* Konev cursed as he continued his search. He loathed the idea of relinquishing one of his classic cars, but he would if it meant getting out of trouble with the troll scholar.

Suddenly, he remembered something in the container of his first haul. He opened the doors and softly patted the Togo Brown 1964 Porsche Cabriolet as he walked past it on his way to the bookshelf in the far corner. There were no books on it, but there was a pair of green aventurine bookends carved like elephants. *What scholar couldn't use bookends?* he reasoned. *It's even made of stone—that's got to resonant with a troll.*

He checked the time. He needed to get on the road if he

wanted to make the most of daylight. He carefully wrapped the elephantine bookends so they wouldn't get damaged in transit and locked up all his containers. Then he secured the barn and grabbed his luggage from the house, putting everything in the back of his Skoda Kodiaq. He pointed the SUV toward Finland and talked himself down before he reached the border guards, who seemed content with his persona of a nature enthusiast visiting for a weekend hike.

Thankful that the eight-hour drive passed without incident, he had just enough time to check into his hotel in Lappeenranta, Finland before his dinner reservations at Nautilus, an establishment overlooking the harbor at Lake Saimaa. Between the stress and travel, he slept hard and didn't rise until after nine. He had a lazy morning and breakfasted in his room before readying his backpack.

When he left his hotel, he looked like the average hiker ready for a day in the great outdoors instead of a highly trained operative about to make a trip into the Magh Meall. In his car, he crossed over several smaller bridges before reaching his destination: one of the numerous peninsulas of a large island owned by the Ivory Tower.

Officially, it was a tree farm—something that wasn't labor intensive and didn't require a constant work force. Konev always timed his personal visits for the weekend when there was virtually no chance of running into the farm employees who periodically cleared the underbrush and made sure everything was growing straight. As for the accidental tourist, it was unlikely. Lake Saimaa was littered with more than 14,000 islands and its coast was mazed by countless peninsulas and channels. There were far more interesting places to see than a tree farm.

He opened the gate and let himself in. As expected, there were no other vehicles parked at the administration building and he had the pick of spaces in the small lot. With his backpack squarely on his shoulders and hips, he hiked toward the back of the farm. Beyond the cultivated growth was a wild area: the perfect place for agents to enter the middle lands.

He found walking between the straight rows of evenly spaced silver birch a little unnerving. The juxtaposition of natural things in an unnatural position was jarring, but once he was out of the farm, the forest was serene with untidy clusters and patches. The ground was pockmocked with the round scars of previous visits by Tower agents over the decades.

When he found a suitable spot, he trenched out a circle large enough for him and his backpack and marked his seat with a towel and a small mechanical clock. Using his compass as a guide, he started placing single seeds of barley at the cardinal directions, then the ordinal directions, and finally the secondary intercardinal directions. Once all sixteen seeds were placed, he downed a bottle of water, ate two power bars, and took out a short sword from his backpack—he wasn't going to enter the land near Duncith unarmed.

At five till noon, he sat down on the towel, closed his eyes, and started chanting. When the clock struck twelve, he started painting his will into the air around him, like doing arcane papier mâché. Eventually, the swatches crossed over one another and formed a pulsating sphere. He continued chanting until the clock struck thirteen.

The pure, sweet smell of the Magh Meall filled his nostrils, but the aroma was spoiled when he opened his eyes and found a pair of goblins eyeing him with amazement—they'd seen humans before, but never one in the act of entering their realm.

"Piss off!" Konev shouted and they jumped like frightened cats. The heavy bags over their curved and hunched shoulders bounced as they hustled down the trail. He stood and slipped on his backpack, following them on the trail that would eventually lead to the cobblestoned road to Duncith.

Duncith was a large city and one of the few in the Magh Meall that practitioners could reach from anywhere on the globe, provided they were willing to burn enough metaphysical energy in travel. He always preferred to make the drive and come at full power because Duncith was *not* a safe place. It was a dolorous den of the despicable, which was why he arrived visibly armed and a little out of the way.

The glooming city was surrounded by a massive ebon wall that towered as tall as the trees, as if it were a natural feature. It was made of stone—or something like stone—and purple tendrils of power crackled through it like the veins of a living thing. Four gates breached the wall at the cardinal directions, each a massive gaping maw. It was hard to tell which gates were carved to resemble some prehistoric beast and which were actual skulls of creatures long-since destroyed in prior epochs, as they all were limned with the same inky coating.

As Konev neared the eldritch city, the traffic increased but the throng of travelers gave him a wide berth on the cobbled road. Here, humans were an oddity, something to be gawked at but also leery of. They cast furtive glances in his direction, but quickly looked away no matter how hard they wanted to stare.

The majority were rural goblins, the underground farmers that wormed their way through the maggot holes that writhed away under the surrounding forest. They were a smallish green-skinned folk, only four feet tall on average. Muscular and bandy legged, they could climb like spiders when on all fours, but the goblins lining up to enter the Syöjätär Gate were here to trade. The massive bags upon their backs and wagons were filled with the strange subterranean foodstuffs that flourished in the absence of light.

On the opposite end of the spectrum were trolls, who were uniformly tall and freakishly strong but varied in shape, thickness, and color befitting their clan. Somewhere between was an array of goblin-kin: blue-tinged kobolds, gray and ashy orcs, and shaggy black-haired bugbears to name a few. They were all very sensitive about their lineage—pity the fool that called any of them goblins.

Skittering between the legs of all these travelers were messenger gremlins, no taller than calf high on a goblin. They were far faster than anything on two legs should be, with the speed and agility of a house cat on thick carpet matched with the boundless endurance of a wolf.

Konev found himself next to a bugbear, a goblin-kin that looked like a Siberian *chuchuna* with protruding lower tusks. He nodded at the creature who gave him a single grunt, an agreement that there was no problem here unless the other brought one. The crowd compressed the closer it moved to the gate, and soon he was just another sojourner. The various occupants came and went but Endless Duncith always remained.

The wall was forty yards tall and half as thick, large enough to block out the warmth of the purple sunlight. As Konev stood in its shadow, he awed at the curved bones of the great Syöjätär skull made hard as stone and black as pitch through some unknown sorcery. Entering the city was like passing through the gullet of the legendary dragon witch herself.

As always, the protective enchantments on the gate tugged and pulled against his personal protections. Human wizards were flagged as persons of interest because as a group they had garnered a reputation for being vexatious, especially those doing business in Duncith. Soon, he would pick up a tail—a personal watcher who'd keep track of him until he left the city—but Konev's destination was only a few blocks from the

Syöjätär Gate. If everything went well, his business would be done before his minder arrived from the castle.

Glumra's shop, Pages from the Troll and Toad, was doubly warded in comparison to the gate and Konev had to push his way through, like walking against a strong wind. The troll scholar had no desire to do business with anyone too weak to enter.

"Good day, wizard," the warty toad-like creature croaked from his guard station by the door. It was Glumra's partner and simply went by Toad, although Konev did not believe that was its name or its species. It had the stench of hell about it.

"Good day to you, Master Toad," Konev responded with a bow. He always gave it an honorific to be on the safe side. Toad's four bulbous eyes moved independent of each other while they rapidly scanned Konev's entire body and aura.

"He's waiting," it croaked and thumbed toward the back of the shop once he passed the screening. "You're lucky. He's in a good mood today."

"Better to be lucky than good," he nervously joked as he walked past.

"Is that you, Konev?" Glumra called from the back. The troll's three sets of vocal cords keyed the question in a cheery major chord.

"It is," he answered as he turned the corner and set eyes on the troll's crusty body.

Glumra was a salt pan troll and a little on the short-side,

barely seven feet tall. However, what he lacked in height he made up in bulk; the troll scholar was on the other side of six hundred pounds at minimum. His stature was simian with a tuft of black hair on the end of his prehensile tail. Resembling a mix between elephant hide and crocodile hide, his skin was a biological crust with deep cracks where insects and small lizards darted and dashed with impunity.

As he greeted Konev, the fissures around his mouth widened with a superficial smile that didn't reach the sharply sloping brow that gave the troll's face its triangular shape. "Do you have it?" he asked, pointing to Konev's backpack. "Let's see it."

Konev kept his distance as he delivered the bad news. "No, it was stolen from me." The troll stood and expanded, causing the tiny creatures living on his skin to scurry inside and causing Konev to jump back. He'd never seen an angry troll puff at such close range. "But I am here to return your advance and I have brought a gift in hopes we can continue to do business together," he quickly added. He fumbled with the buckles of his bag and removed the aventurine bookends. "A set of two." He stretched and put both on the counter.

Konev held his breath as Glumra grabbed one in each enormous hand. The troll spun them about and then returned them to the worn wood of the desk. "And the advance?" he asked in a chromatic cluster that grated a musical ear.

"Certainly!" Konev replied. He withdrew five gold coins from his backpack and handed them to Glumra. He checked each one for the stamp of Duncith; the city minted its own currency as precious metals were one of the few things that could travel between the mortal lands and the Magh Meall with almost no karmic cost.

The troll un-puffed and sat back down. He beckoned Konev to approach with a large finger. "Tell me what happened." The minor chord was at least tonal, which Konev took as a positive sign—Glumra wasn't going to kill him. Yet.

He gave the abbreviated version that cast no blame upon himself and ended with a profuse apology. "I am extremely sorry. I've never failed before. I only discovered the theft yesterday, otherwise I would have notified you earlier."

Glumra vibrated as he *himmmed* and *hummmed* his way to a decision. Other trolls would have immediately ripped off the puny human's head or rent him in two, but he was a scholar and prided himself on being reasonable. "Konev, I like you. We have done well together and as you said, you haven't let me down before. I understand these things happen." But then his three-note voice turned unharmonious and his countenance stern. "But if it happens again, Toad will gut you, stuff you, and mount you on the wall as a cautionary tale for others who promise but do not deliver. Do you understand what I am saying?"

"Yes, sir," Konev answered with military precision. "Thank you for your understanding."

His crusty features softened. "Thank you for these." The

troll ran his fingers over the bookends. "They are nice. I know just where to put them."

Chapter Twenty-One

The transition from pavement to gravel rumbled under the wheels of Major Alexander Lukin's Lada Niva. His gloved hands randomly tapped against the steering wheel as he guided the vehicle around the final two turns before arriving at the gate to the Tower's tree farm. He checked his watch before proceeding. It wouldn't do to arrive too early and let Konev know he was here before he entered the Magh Meall.

When he opened the gate, he spotted the Skoda Kodiaq in the parking lot and parked alongside it. Even if he hadn't recognized the plates as Konev's, the tracker Lukin had placed underneath the back bumper confirmed it. He removed the bug before heading south.

There were places like this in Russia—sparsely inhabited, filled with trees and water—but the Finnish air smelled fresh and full of promise. He wondered if it was really so different than his home country or if it was psychological. The grass was always greener on the other side, as the Americans said.

His report to General Secretary Yastrzhembsky had been

received without comment, but the funds to cover his expenses were transferred without delay. Lukin had heard nothing of the matter trickle down from higher ups, which was hardly surprising. By his reckoning, Volsky had decided to continue to shield Konev and any political damage his golden boy might have suffered was buffeted by the chairman's very large umbrella. There would be an official investigation into the theoretical leaks that would inevitably come up blank because no one wanted there to be an internal mole. Volsky may be unsteady on his perch, but he was still atop it and therefore had the rule of the roost.

He sighed. *Which makes all of us chickens running around with their heads cut off.* In his opinion, this was the bigger problem. Institutional inertia made enacting change slow and difficult, and that allowed bad leadership to continue leading poorly. That could only lead to two scenarios: apathy taking over and the rot setting in completely, or resentment and frustration that boiled over until it passed a tipping point. Only then did change occur, often swiftly and violently.

Lukin cleared the rows of planted trees for the wild area a few minutes after one o'clock. If Konev had done the ritual correctly, he and all his possessions would be in the middle lands, so Lukin searched by looking for a shovel or newly trenched circle among the wild growth. When he found what he was looking for, he took cover behind a tree ten meters south and drew his MP-443 Grach. All he had to do was wait for Konev's return. He paused to say a variant of the age-old prayer of all field operatives—*may the law of numbers not turn against me*—and began his vigil.

Eventually, a rogue breeze dropped from the sky, and with it, Konev in the center of the circle. "Captain Konev," Lukin greeted him cordially from behind.

The address instantly put Konev on alert: he'd told no one he was coming here. He spun around and saw the 9mm pointing at him. "Major Lukin," Konev responded cautiously as he froze in place. Were he closer, the younger man might have taken a gamble, but Lukin was ten meters away from him—out of range for a physical attack but close enough to make Konev a sitting duck.

"What's in the backpack?" Lukin asked without lowering his gun.

"Nothing important," Konev replied a little too quickly.

"I'll be the judge of that," Lukin chided him like a naughty child. "Throw it to your left as far as you can. If it's less than three meters, I'll assume you don't want to keep on living."

Konev slipped off the backpack and heaved it as far as he could, which was considerably easier since it no longer held two stone bookends. "What is this all about?" he ventured a question.

"The higher ups believe you were not completely honest in your mission reports," Lukin told the truth deceptively.

"Volsky?" Konev blurted out, incredulously. He couldn't

imagine the chairman sending Lukin to take him in. He thoroughly disliked "the German," as he called Lukin in private.

Lukin chose not to correct him. "Who else?" He savored the pained look on Konev's face as it passed from disbelief to betrayal. He rubbed a little salt in the wound. "The chairman knows when to cash in his chips and leave the table. How long did you think he'd keep protecting you when you were lying to him?"

"I've done nothing wrong," Konev insisted.

Lukin barked a cruel laugh. "Of course you haven't. Lieutenant Lokhov's phone must have mysteriously tossed itself back into the Sûre." Konev kept his expression blank at Lukin's revelation, but he couldn't stop the color draining from his face as panic descended. *Shit, shit, shit! How much do they know?*

"I have no idea what you're talking about," he categorically denied it. "This is all just a misunderstanding."

"Come now, *bratishka*, we have no time for these games," Lukin replied in patronizing tone. "Slowly stand up and turn away from me. Put your hands behind your back." Konev complied; being taken in was better than being shot.

"I've wanted to say this for a long time, Mikhail, and now seems appropriate," Lukin said, sharing his real internal state briefly. "Your attitude and disregard is a discredit to everything my parents built. Say hi to Volsky for me when he joins you in Hell." Before Konev could react, Lukin's Grach roared, nearly severing Konev's head from his body. The captain flopped to the ground like a gutted fish.

Lukin stayed still, listening to the echo of the gunshot dissipate and waiting to see if anyone else came to investigate. When the forest remained quiet, he holstered his weapon and slid a pair of polypropylene anti-skid covers over his shoes before getting any closer. From the breast pocket of his jacket, he extracted a small plastic bag. Inside was an expended Salt Mine bullet he'd been saving for just such an occasion.

He opened the bag and held the spent bullet by the plastic, lodging it into the bloodiest part of what remained of Konev's neck. The Finnish forensic techs would assume the bullet found in the neck was the one that caused the damage, especially since it was the same caliber as his MP-443. When the Ivory Tower did its own analysis, the bullet's unusual appearance and composition would get flagged as Salt Mine in origin. They didn't know how it worked, but they did have a full metallurgical breakdown for comparison.

Lukin smirked. *Thanks for the assist, Wilson.* Were it not for the pot shot Wilson had taken at him in Tripoli, he would not have had this opportunity. As soon as Konev's death was attributed to the Salt Mine, the failure at Schlass Wollef would also be attributed to them. It was consistent with his report to the general secretary and Konev's own report. More importantly, it allowed Volsky to declare there was no leak in Russian intelligence.

As extra insurance, Lukin withdrew three packets of salt taken from his hotel's breakfast buffet this morning and spread their contents around the general area of the circle, particularly on the dry parts of the body. It might be days before the body was found and there was no guarantee it wouldn't rain before then, but if the salt was found, it further pointed the finger away from him and in the wrong direction.

With the crime scene finished, he walked to Konev's backpack. Lukin had to leave the Skoda to ensure the body would be found, but the backpack could disappear. "Let's see what goodies we have in here."

Chapter Twenty-Two

Maastricht Underground, The Netherlands
22nd of September, 2:43 a.m. (GMT+2)

Underneath the city of Maastricht was a labyrinth of caves stretching over 300 kilometers long, and somewhere along one of its 23,000 passages rested a piece of Voynich manuscript. At least, that was what the enchanted words on Haddock's skin was telling him.

He held out his left hand at the junction and waited for one branch to vibrate more than another. Dot had written out the same message as before—*Find me*—only this time it was in the same ink as the Voynich manuscript, albeit it a fresh batch with the ingredients he and Martinez had acquired. The boost in range was impressive, but it wasn't as simple as following a dousing rod to water. The geography of caves and tunnels stacked on top of each other made it more challenging than finding a slip of paper in a shipping container. After more than a few false starts, double-backs, and circumnavigations, he had the impression he was close.

"This way," he motioned to the right and Moncrief followed with an electric lantern and enchanted string. Dot's *Find me* was a fine guide coming in, but the neverending ball of twine was their mechanical exit strategy.

"We've got to be close," she whispered. "I'm getting goose bumps." They had long ago left the tourist routes and the profoundly heavy darkness crept along the edge of their light and devoured the echo of her voice.

She reached down for Carnwennan, sheathed in its bejeweled red-leather scabbard slung on her hip. She'd had more brushes with danger than her years should allow and had developed a good intuition for these things. Even though the caves of Maastricht had never been used as a tomb, that didn't mean there wasn't danger lurking in the limestone corridors.

"Are you getting soft on me?" he teased her to cut the tension. He'd helped train Moncrief when she'd first signed on to the Salt Mine; sending the heiress to the Farm or any other official operative training would have compromised her cover as a bubbly socialite.

The feel of her preferred weapon's hilt bolstered her courage and she gave him a sharp look. "As if! Don't forget, I'm your ride home."

They followed the passage as it twisted and turned until they hit a dead end. "Another double back?" she asked.

He shook his head. "No, not this time. Every fiber of my hand is telling me it's behind that wall."

She sweetly smiled until her dimples reached maximum depth. "Then it's a good thing I always come prepared." She hung the lantern on her belt and tucked the ball of twine in her pocket before pulling out a miner's pick from her backpack. "This will let us walk through any solid material except salt."

Haddock bent down and kissed the top of her head. "You are a gem."

"I know." She coquettishly shrugged before getting down to the brass tacks. "We both have to have our hands on it if we want to pass through and in case I am out of it, the activation phrase is 'ain't no miner like a 49er.'"

He snorted. "Seriously?"

"Don't look at me. I didn't make it up. It was made around the time of the California gold rush." She took Carnwennan out of its sheath. "Just in case. We don't know what's on the other side."

"That's not a bad idea," he agreed as he pulled a bat from his forearm. With their hands on the pick, they stepped through the limestone. The light from the lantern flooded the room on the other side of the wall, catching the edge of a massive sword in midair. He saw the blade in time to let go of the pick, push Moncrief to one side, and jump to the other. The owner of the sword was a tall figure dressed in black medieval armor brandishing a sword and shield, and the clang of the metal as it hit the stone floor bounced off the stone walls.

There was no light save the electric lantern that had fallen off Moncrief's belt, casting shadows at odd angles from the floor. It was enough for Haddock to get his bearings. The chamber was no bigger than ten by ten and he didn't see an exit. A flat surface had been carved out of the rock but there was no other furniture.

How did this guy get in here? he wondered as he picked up the other end of his bat and used it defensively as another blow came at him. Moncrief was already invisible—Carnwennan allowed her to bend light like the fae—and if he'd taught her anything during her training, she was looking for a chink in warrior's armor.

Sweep the leg! Haddock roared in his mind as he swung and hit low on the calf, hoping to knock the armored warrior off balance. The ebony figure howled, but he didn't go down. Moncrief took the opportunity to stab her dagger into the warrior's sword arm, targeting the gap between the cuirass and the metal covering the upper arm. Unfortunately it wedged in and it was torn from her grasp as he stumbled in pain, but did not fall. Instead, he dropped his shield and reached to pull the dagger out of his shoulder.

Great, I'm going to die in a Monty Python meme, he morbidly mused as he dropped the bat and pushed up his sleeve to access the gun tattooed on his forearm. Now without her dagger, Moncrief followed suit, reaching for her holster.

The warrior dropped his sword and took a knee as soon as he saw Haddock extract the weapon from ink on his skin. He raised his empty hands into the air and a deep voice rumbled from within the helmet. "I yield, magician! I yield!"

Moncrief and Haddock, who had him covered at ten and two, exchanged looks, uncertain what to do next. "If you yield, slide your sword and shield to the far wall," she ordered. The warrior was not accustomed to taking orders from women, but there was the undeniable tenor of rule in her voice.

He complied and tried to explain. "I thought you were thieves. It had been so long, I had given up hope of being relieved."

Haddock gave diplomacy a shot. "Now that we know we are not enemies, we can tend to your wounds. Be still; my friend will pull the dagger out of your shoulder." He nodded to Moncrief, letting her know he still had her covered.

She holstered her gun and retrieved Carnwennan. As she cleaned off the blood, the warrior took off his helmet at the sight of the dagger. His face was as black as his armor and he lowered his bare head before her slight figure. "Had I known you were an emissary of the king, I would never have attacked."

Haddock put the pieces together—Carnwennan was Arthur's dagger, the full suit of armor, a black knight in the lowlands… "Arise, Moriaen," he ventured an educated guess.

The knight smiled; long had it been since he'd heard another call him by name. "You know of me."

"I have heard the songs sung of your heroic deeds," Haddock answered, listing the Arthurian romances he could remember. "The search for your father, your adventures with Walewein, Lancelot and Gawain, your valiant attempt to fight off the Saxons and Irish."

Referring to old times and friends past deepened Moriaen's bittersweet grin. "That was many lifetimes ago."

"And yet you are here with us," Haddock remarked. "There must be magic afoot."

The knight pulled off his gloves and showed them his bare hands. The ink blended in with his dark skin but was quite visible on his lighter palms. "The word is with me and it has sustained me."

Haddock's left hand itched like crazy as he examined Moriaen hands. *Holy shit, he's the missing quire…or rather, the missing quire was written on him.* He hadn't seen that coming, but it made sense. He regularly inked his skin and vellum was animal skin. "How far does this writing go?"

"Down my arms and across my chest," he answered. "You are the new guardian, aren't you?"

Haddock nodded. "Yes, but I need to make room." He immediately put Dot's *Find me* back on the scrap of parchment it had originally been written on and sighed as he experienced a moment of relief from the itching. Moriaen stared in wonder. He wasn't a practitioner himself, just a man who had made an oath; a canvas for the magic of others.

"Perhaps you can tell us how you came to protect it while I move some things around," Haddock suggested as he took off his jacket and shirt to strategically move tattoos from his arms to other parts of his body.

"Forgive me, I have grown unaccustomed to the company of others," Moriaen apologized and sheepishly averted his eyes. "As you have heard of some my exploits, I will start my account later. After I found my father, he returned to marry my mother and together we reclaimed the country and ruled well, first my parents, then myself."

"One day, an old friend called upon me. Merlin the Enchanter had one final quest from Arthur. At first, I thought it was impossible. Arthur was dead. I and all the remaining knights that served him had mourned his passing. But then, the wizard told me about the prophecy—"

"The return of the king," Moncrief guessed.

Moriaen gave a look of shock that quickly turned into a knowing nod. "Of course, you must have heard of it, maiden of Arthur." Moncrief bit her tongue but not before rolling her eyes after the knight turned to address Haddock. "I have been its keeper but I cannot read it. Can you tell me what it says?"

Haddock shook his head. "No, I cannot read it either, but I know someone who can."

Moriaen's countenance relaxed. "Then my time wasn't in vain." He suddenly felt the weight of his burden. "I have one request, before you take the words from me. Long have I been the black knight, but I think I would like to pass from this world as only a man. Could you help me out of my armor?" he asked Haddock.

"Of course," Haddock replied, and motioned for Moncrief

to help as well. Taking off a full suit of armor took an inordinate amount of time with many individual pieces connected by straps and buckles.

"I feel lighter already," Moriaen joked as he took a seat on the platform that had acted as his bed, seat, and desk. The faithful knight had kept his covenant and welcomed a measure of rest. "I am ready."

Haddock took Moriaen's large hands into his. As the scribe applied his will, the dark ink drained from the Moorish knight onto Haddock's skin, starting on his right hand, scrolling up his right arm, across his upper chest, and down his left arm. As the last of the enchanted ink left his body, Moriaen exhaled his final words. They were so soft, they were almost inaudible, but Haddock heard them.

He held on to his hands even though there was no more magic to absorb, and he bid him goodbye. "Farewell Moriaen, son of Perceval, and faithful knight of Camelot."

He crossed Moriaen's hands over his body and Moncrief laid his sword and shield beside him.

"What did he say, at the end?" Moncrief asked him.

"*Inna lillahi wa inna ilayhi raji'un,*" he replied in Arabic. "Verily we belong to Allah, and truly to Him shall we return." He got dressed and started rubbing his arms against each other. "Let's get back to the Mine. The sooner this ink is off me, the better."

"Is it that bad?" she asked sympathetically.

"It's like being infested by scabies, but only after catching chicken pox the day after you rolled around in a patch of poison ivy," he replied.

"Jeffery will have something on the plane," she stated her confidence in her steward. Her private jet was parked at Maastricht Aachen Airport just outside the city. "If nothing else, he can make you a mean drink and tape oven mitts to your hands to keep you from scratching after you've passed out."

"God bless Jeffery," he declared as he put his hand on the pick and they passed through the limestone wall.

She handed him the ball of twine. "Wind this up. It will keep your hands busy so you won't scratch." In the dark tunnels by the light of the electric lantern, he found the coarse twine was just right for scratching between his fingers.

Epilogue

Detroit, Michigan, USA
22nd of September, 7:12 a.m. (GMT-4)

Leader took the elevator into the secure storage area well below the library. Moncrief had brought in Stigma via the freight elevator just in case Merlin's magic had corrupted him, and Chloe and Dot started the magical extraction as soon as he'd arrived. She passed through the eldritch doors of silver and gold and down the long hall before arriving at the designed saferoom. When she arrived, only the librarians were inside, hunched over a sheet of vellum covered in ink. The lone lamp had been positioned in front of them so their shadows wouldn't get in each other's light.

"Where's Stigma?" Leader asked as she crossed the threshold and pointed to the empty cot.

"LaSalle took him topside thirty minutes ago," Chloe updated her.

"How is he?" Leader inquired.

"He's fine," Dot reassured her, "although you wouldn't know it from his bellyaching."

"LaSalle scanned him before and after extraction and gave him the green light. The steroid shot relieved much of the residual itching. He'll be slathered in emollients for the foreseeable future, but he should bounce back quickly," Chloe gave her the long answer.

"And this is what he had on him," Leader surmised. She stepped next to Chloe, careful not to block the light. "What am I looking at?"

"Quire eighteen of the Voynich manuscript, AKA the Morcandian Key," Dot replied, but her tone suggested frustration instead of victory.

Leader asked for it straight. "What's the bad news?"

"It lost its formatting," Dot grumbled.

"I'm going to need more than that," Leader said after failing to parse the cryptic response on her own.

"Merlin transferred the original to Moriaen's skin, Stigma moved it to his skin, and then it got moved again to this parchment," Chloe explained. "All the writing and magic is still there, but there are no paragraphs, page breaks, or column widths to help guide how it should be laid out on a page. Without knowing the dimensions of the original quire, we can't use quire sixteen to decode it, and that's assuming Merlin didn't do anything tricky with the word placement."

"Well, what can you ascertain from its current state?" Leader asked diplomatically.

"We think it's a ribbon map," Chloe responded. "A set of

travel instructions on how to get from point A to point B with regard to only the things you're supposed to encounter along the path but nothing else."

"So we have instructions that we can't read," Leader summed up their position.

Dot grinned. "Ah, but I do know point A and point B. They're the first and last words of the quire: the mortal realm to the counter earth."

"The hypothesized parallel planet opposite Earth's trajectory that we can't see because it's on the other side of the sun?" Leader guffawed. "I thought physics and astronomy had ruled out the existence of counter earth."

Dot shrugged. "I'm only reporting what I'm reading."

"According to Moncrief and Haddock, Merlin was going to use this for the return of Arthur," Chloe filled her in.

"But he could have just been saying that to get Moriaen to agree to hold onto it," Dot added.

Leader rubbed her temples. "Should we warn Vivian, maybe suggest she check in on Merlin in case we've inadvertently triggered a prophesy?" No one knew where the lady of the lake kept her former teacher, only that he was imprisoned.

"It might lead to her to discovering Arthur and Excalibur are no longer in Avalon," Chloe voiced her concern.

"But if we tell her, she won't suspect us," Dot offered her take.

Chloe nodded. "She makes a good point."

Leader knew what she had to do. When the twins were on the same page, it was usually the right course of action. "Okay, let's move upstairs and figure out what to say over coffee," she agreed.

Dot perked up. "Coffee?!"

"I picked up a carton with some pastries on my way in," Leader informed them. "It's waiting for us on the sixth floor."

THE END

The agents of The Salt Mine will return in *Dark Matter*

Printed in Great Britain
by Amazon